A Spy
Unmasked

A Spy Unmasked

an In the Crown's Secret Service novel

Tina Gabrielle

This book is a work of fiction. Names, characters, places, and incidents are the product of the author's imagination or are used fictitiously. Any resemblance to actual events, locales, or persons, living or dead, is coincidental.

Copyright © 2014 by Tina Sickler. All rights reserved, including the right to reproduce, distribute, or transmit in any form or by any means. For information regarding subsidiary rights, please contact the Publisher.

Entangled Publishing, LLC
2614 South Timberline Road
Suite 109
Fort Collins, CO 80525
Visit our website at www.entangledpublishing.com.

Scandalous is an imprint of Entangled Publishing, LLC.

Edited by Terese Ramin
Cover design by Libby Murphy

ISBN 978-1502915061

Manufactured in the United States of America

First Edition November 2014

For Laura & Gabrielle.
May you always reach for the stars.
I love you.

Chapter One

May 10, 1820
London, Viscount Delmont's ballroom

Robert Ware adjusted his black half mask and sipped a glass of claret as he surveyed the glittering ballroom. Tonight was supposed to be an ordinary mission, similar to the countless other clandestine operations he had carried out.

The Delmonts' masquerades were rumored to be quite dissolute, and from the look of the guests this party lived up to that reputation. Well past midnight, expensive champagne continued to flow freely. A voluptuous blonde with a dazzling diamond necklace and a vast amount of cleavage boldly met his eyes and licked her painted lips.

Robert grinned and raised his glass in silent salute. *Ah, for king and country,* he mused.

A liveried footman carrying a silver tray halted beside him. "Viscount Delmont's guards are now making the rounds in his private wing," the man whispered.

Robert swapped the claret for a flute of champagne from the server's tray without making eye contact with him.

Ian MacDonald was a fellow agent assigned to observe Lord Delmont's men while Robert carried out his assignment. Unobtrusive, of average height and build with brown hair and eyes, Ian easily blended in with a crowd.

"How much time will I have?" Robert asked.

"A half hour."

A half hour. Little time to retrieve the package and quit the place before the guards made their next rotation.

A booming laugh drew Robert's attention. Lord Delmont stood in the corner of the ballroom. He was unmasked and talking to three other men. As the head of the London Inventors' Society, the viscount's interests lay in chemistry. He was a bear of a man with a chest the size of a small armoire, meaty hands, and a short neck that gave him the appearance that his head rested directly upon his shoulders. By the look of Delmont's florid complexion and glassy eyes, he was well on his way to being drunk.

"I wonder what he says about the murders," Robert murmured.

"You mean to speak to the man? That's not part of the plan."

"He's not the mastermind behind the killings."

Ian focused his gaze over Robert's shoulder. "You'll have to wait for another opportunity to engage Delmont. The guards have returned to the ballroom."

Time to go. Robert drained his glass, placed it on Ian's tray and slipped out of the crowded ballroom into the hall. Voices of revelers echoed off the black-and-white Italian marble floor, crystal clinked, and a woman's trill of laughter followed.

He smiled at a group of bejeweled ladies and made a show of heading for the ornately carved staircase leading outside. As soon as the group passed, he turned right into Delmont's private wing. He paused to allow his eyes to adjust from the brightness of the ballroom chandeliers to the low-burning candles in wall sconces that dimly illuminated the corridor. Gilt-framed portraits of the viscount's ancestors peered down at him with haughty disdain as he moved past. He ventured farther, his footsteps muffled by the thick Brussels runner.

The library occupied the last door on the right. He had memorized the layout of the mansion weeks ago, as soon as Wendover, his superior at the Home Office, had advised him of the mission—one for which Robert had been handpicked.

Crack the safe. Retrieve Delmont's documents. If you are apprehended, the Crown will deny your involvement.

All things Robert knew. His unexpected and recently inherited title from his uncle—the Earl of Kirkland—could not change his past. He was a soldier in an invisible army. He would never be a decorated war hero. There were no medals, no accolades for men like him.

He reached the library and opened the door an inch.

Empty.

Slipping inside, he quietly closed the door. Moonlight through the French doors behind a rosewood pedestal desk partly illuminated the room. It would have to be sufficient as he dared not light a lamp.

He scanned the space, his mind calculating where a safe might be hidden. Behind a priceless Rembrandt painting. Beneath the parquet floor under the desk. Perhaps behind a false stone in the mantle.

He found it built into a tall mahogany bookshelf. The gilded spines of the books gave it away. A complete set of Johnathan Swift's first-edition treasures. A rarity, indeed.

Pushing the books aside, he ran his fingers along the inside of the shelf until he felt a latch. There was a slight click when he pressed it and a panel swung open to reveal a formidable strongbox of hardwood with steel bands. His lips curled in a smile as he reached out to caress the lock.

"Ah, a Richmond Company lock," he whispered reverently.

He must use nondestructive manipulation. No one must suspect the safe had been tampered with until Lord Delmont went to retrieve his treasonous documents.

Robert withdrew his lock picks from his pocket and went to work.

Fifteen minutes later the safe was open and he stared at a pile of banknotes six inches thick and a fortune in rubies and diamonds.

He reached past the banknotes and jewels to retrieve a battered, leather-bound ledger and a sheaf of papers from the back of the safe. Tucking them inside the jacket pocket of his blue superfine, he closed the safe and secured the panel.

He was arranging the books in their precise order when he heard a rustle of clothing outside the door.

Bloody hell.

Slipping behind the end of the bookshelf, he reached for the blade in his boot just as the library door cracked open. He clutched one of the books in his left hand, preparing to throw it, when a figure entered the room.

"Who's there?"

A woman's voice.

She came forward, slowly stepping into a swath of moonlight until her features were fully illuminated.

His first impression struck him like a blow to the gut: *she does not belong here.* She was tall and slim and possessed a wild beauty. Among the garishly dressed women in the ballroom, she would stand out like fine Italian glass beside rough-cut jars.

She had fiery red hair. Odd, he'd never found females with such bright hair attractive. But this one was different. She wore a peacock-feathered mask and a turquoise gown. Her bodice was low, though nothing as vulgar as the other female guests in attendance. Yet it was her eyes that drew him. Not blue, as he would have expected with the flame-colored hair, but a mesmerizing green that glittered like emeralds from the slits of her mask.

He paused, slipping the knife back into his boot before stepping away from the shelf.

"Who are you?" she called out.

He assumed an air of nonchalance. "Merely a guest of Lord Delmont's," he said, advancing toward her.

Full lips parted, then closed, and she raised a pistol that had been hidden in the folds of her skirts. "Please do not move. I'm not afraid to use this," she said, aiming the pistol at him.

He concealed his surprise. Her grip on the weapon was firm, but her voice was not. Could she be working for Delmont?

He hadn't believed the viscount was solely responsible for the secretive agenda behind the Inventors' Society. Robert had suspected a mastermind behind the murders, but never had he thought a woman was involved.

He flashed his most charming smile. "Careful," he

murmured. "Is it loaded?"

"Of course it's loaded," she snapped.

"What's your name?" he asked.

"What's yours?"

"As we are both masked, let's keep it mysterious. You may call me Robert."

"All right," she said. "What are you doing in here, Robert?"

"I needed to escape the heat and noise of the ballroom."

"That's what the terrace is for."

"*Ah,* but I thought to read."

She glanced at the book in his hand. "*Gulliver's Travels?* I'd hardly mark you as a man inclined to read Swift."

"How intriguing. What type of man do you believe I am?"

"A false one. Are you one of Viscount Delmont's spies?"

"A spy? I have no idea what you mean. I already told you. I'm a guest."

His eyes narrowed, and he studied her more closely. If she was employed by Delmont, then she would have known he was not. So who the hell was she?

"You're lying." She jerked her head in the direction of the bookshelf. "What's there?"

He shrugged. "Books."

Keeping the pistol aimed at him, she went to the bookshelf and moved one of the books.

The false panel was in place and was sufficient to conceal the strongbox.

Unless one knew what to look for.

Robert contemplated a swift blow to the head, nothing to cause permanent harm, just enough to render her unconscious. But if she wasn't working for Delmont, then that would leave her at the mercy of his ruthless guards.

With an unladylike oath beneath her breath, she whirled back to him. "Did you find what you were searching for?" she said.

Her eyes, visible through the openings in her mask, betrayed her fear. He could almost hear the pounding of blood in her veins. He was skilled at reading people, not only the truth behind their words, but their visceral physical reactions, and she was scared.

Scared and desperate.

"I don't know what you're talking about," he said.

Biting her bottom lip, she cocked the hammer. "Show me your pockets."

This was getting out of hand. His voice hardened. "Give me the gun before it accidently fires. This isn't a game."

She raised her chin in defiance. "A game! I'll fire if I'm forced to. Now give me what you've stolen."

"You don't intend to hurt anyone," he said.

"How do you know my intentions?"

"My intuition tells me you are in over your head."

"Then your intuition is wrong."

His laughter had a sharp edge. "When it comes to life and limb, I'm never wrong."

He stepped closer until he was within inches of the barrel of the pistol.

Her hand trembled. "No closer. Please…"

"Lady, we must leave here. It's not safe."

She shook her head. "Not until you hand over what you've stolen."

A door opened and closed at the far end of the corridor. Male voices followed.

Damnation.

A swift glance at the minute hand on the long case clock in the corner of the room told him they were running out of time.

The woman must have heard it, too. A glazed look of panic shone in her eyes. "Show me!"

The voices were closer now, just outside the library door. It was too late; one of Delmont's guards would be upon them within seconds.

The handle on the door turned…

In one smooth motion, he pushed her hand aside, grasped the pistol from her fingers, and jerked her into his arms. "Not a sound," he ordered.

She gasped in alarm as the door burst open, and Robert lowered his head and swooped down to capture her lips.

Chapter Two

Sophia Merrill had seconds to comprehend it all. He roughly wrapped his arm around her waist and pulled her against a mainmast of solid, male muscle. Through the black half mask she could make out brilliant blue eyes, their color like polished sapphires, and then his mouth covered hers with commanding mastery. Beneath the hardness of his lips she felt instantly overwhelmed and overpowered. The heat from his body enveloped her; the faint scent of his cologne coiled about her. Heart fluttering wildly, she raised her palms to press against his chest.

The door slammed against the wall.

"What are you two doing in here?" a male voice boomed.

Delmont's guard was a bald, brawny man with a square jaw and a bulbous nose.

Sophia jerked in alarm, but the arms of her tawny-haired captor tightened around her waist. Glancing down, he gave her a pointed keep-your-mouth-shut look.

Then he turned to the guard, and a guiltless smile curved his lips. "Ah, the lady and I desired a bit of privacy." Slurring his speech, he sounded like a guest who had made one too many trips to the punch bowl.

Masking her surprise, she went along with the ruse. Her position was precarious, and even if she did not know what his motives were, her own were not innocent, nothing she desired to be brought to Viscount Delmont's attention. Her disguise, the red wig and mask, wouldn't fool the viscount for long, and her identity was something she couldn't risk revealing.

For some reason, this mysterious man—the man who had called himself Robert—was bent on protecting her.

Or himself.

She stole a glance up at him. He was tall and although she was not petite, he made her feel small as he held her tightly against him. He cocked his head to the side, his tawny hair changing in the shafts of moonlight—blond, light brown, then darker—slightly longer than fashion dictated.

The guard hesitated, his eyes narrowing to slits. "How did you get in here? This wing is prohibited."

Robert hiccuped and swayed. "Pardon our intrusion. How does the saying go? Lovers will find a way?"

Her legs shook so badly she feared she would have fallen if not for the arm lashed around her waist. Yet he showed no sign of anxiety or tension. Rather he was like a chameleon, an actor of great skill, able to change his demeanor, his personality, his very essence in order to adapt to his environment.

One thing was clear: he was not one of Delmont's men. The guard would have known him, or worse, Robert would have turned her over to Delmont himself at this first opportunity.

Then who on earth was he?

The guard smirked. His gaze boldly swept over her body and lingered at her breasts. "I don't blame you, my lord, but you'll have to leave, nonetheless."

Robert made a jovial wave with his hand. "We shall return to the ballroom at once."

He released his hold on her waist to clutch her hand. When he led her around the end of the rosewood desk, she intended to follow him straight out the library door, but tripped on an object. Glancing down, she saw the leather-bound copy of *Gulliver's Travels,* which must have dropped when he jerked her into his arms. She immediately tried to hide the incriminating novel with a swish of her skirts.

It was too late. The guard's eyes narrowed speculatively as he spotted the book.

"Stop!" He barreled toward them.

Robert moved so fast, his fists blurred. His swift punch to the guard's stomach caused the man to double over.

She shrieked and leaped to the side as the guard charged headfirst for Robert, sending both men down. The pistol clattered across the parquet floor. They wrestled for control of the weapon; an end table toppled and a lamp shattered.

The deafening *crack* of the pistol firing resounded through the room.

For a heart-stopping moment, she feared Robert had been hit.

Then he rose with the pistol in his hand. Blood flowed from the guard's chest and began pooling on the floor.

Shouts sounded and were followed by screams from panicked guests in the vestibule.

"Good God!" she shrieked. "Is he dead?"

He grasped her arms and shook her. "Are you going to faint?"

"No!"

"Good, because we have seconds before more guards arrive."

He caught her hand and pulled her to the French doors behind the desk. Throwing them open, he dragged her into the back gardens.

A thousand questions rose in her mind, but self-preservation outweighed her curiosity.

Escape.

She had to escape before she was captured and murdered.

Just like Father.

"Move!" He started to run, pulling her with him.

Clutching her skirts in one hand, she followed as he headed away from the manicured lawns, toward the wooded acreage separating the mansion from town.

Her voluminous skirts hindered her, and sharp stones bit into the dainty soles of her ballroom slippers. A drizzling rain had begun to fall, leaving the grass wet, and she slipped. His hold was like an iron manacle about her wrist, catching her before she fell.

Shouts sounded from the open library doors. "In here!"

"He's dead!" another called out.

"Find them!"

She could hear the screams of panicked guests as they fled from the ballroom and crowded together on the front lawn.

Robert and Sophia sprinted past a fountain, stone benches, marble statues of Roman gods and goddesses. Running past a formal maze, they made it through the tended section of the gardens, and reached a dense copse of trees.

They continued to run, weaving through tall elm and oak trees.

The terrain was wild here, and brambles snagged her skirts. Sticks snapped beneath her slippers, and she was forced to leap over low brush. Her chest heaved in her tight bodice, and her breaths came in rasps.

"Hurry. We're almost there," he said.

Almost where? she wanted to ask, but she couldn't catch her breath quickly enough to speak. She knew Delmont's property stretched for a half mile more, up to the back road. Did he plan to hire a hackney and disappear into the London streets?

Shouts sounded through the woods. She glanced back to see a dozen blazing torches weaving among the trees.

Her panic rose to fever pitch. Delmont's guards were gaining ground. A surge of energy, fueled by fear, made her dash onward.

Robert's fingers tightened on her wrist, halting her.

"This way," he said.

He headed not in the direction of the back road, but east, where the dense forest foliage opened up to reveal a small river, its banks lined with stones and soft earth. Here they would be out in the open, completely at the mercy of the pack of men hunting them.

She resisted. "They'll see us!"

"No. Trust me."

Trust him?

Sophia stared up at him. Moonlight gleamed in his eyes through the mask. Gone were both the charming thief she had interrupted and the intoxicated coxcomb the guard had confronted. He now gave the appearance of a soldier, from his broad shoulders, to the firm set of his chiseled jaw, to his deep voice. He had an unmistakable air of efficiency, and the thought struck her that he was used to issuing commands, used to obedience.

A dangerous man.

Angry shouts sounded closer. She could hear the snapping of branches as men tore through the forest.

Panic welled in her throat as the torches bobbed closer and closer.

She turned back to the woods—not entirely safe, yet far safer than this. There tall trees and an abundance of bushes and foliage left dark shadows where a person could hide.

"Let's part ways here," she said.

"No. You'll never make it." His voice was like steel wrapped in silk.

Her options were limited. To resist meant wasting precious time battling him, or she could acquiesce and plan her escape when they were no longer being hunted.

He stepped forward; she didn't shrink from his grasp.

Moments later they reached the riverbank, and he let forth a low whistle. A rider emerged from the trees, holding the reins of a trailing chestnut horse. Her eyes widened at the man's liveried clothing bearing a large *D* representing the Delmont household.

"The lady rides with me, Ian," Robert said in a voice of authority.

"The marquess is not going to like this," the footman said.

"He has no choice."

She glanced from one man to the other. He had a man

inside the viscount's household working for him. Why? Who was he?

She barely had time to ponder the question before Robert lifted her onto the back of the chestnut and mounted behind her.

"Hold on," he said. "We're in for a wild ride."

With a swift kick of his heels, the horse took off at a run. Pressed against his solid chest, she clutched the pommel as they wove through the dense woods at a reckless pace.

Chapter Three

Sophia's thoughts were a jumble of panic and confusion. The guards' shouts faded along with the light from their torches as she and Robert raced through Delmont's property.

Low-hanging branches snarled her skirts and silk stockings. All the while, she was conscious of the places where his body touched hers, of his arms around her as he held the horse's reins, and the occasional jolt of his thigh brushing her hip. The heat from his exertions seeped into her, and her heart pounded in an erratic rhythm. She struggled to shut out any awareness of him.

Think, Sophia!

She had made a dreadful mistake. She had failed in her plan to secure the evidence needed to arrest Viscount Delmont. She would have been better off walking into the ballroom and shooting the blackguard with her pistol.

Her position was precarious. She was in the clutches of a dangerous mystery man whose motives were unknown. One thing was certain. He was not searching for a book to read during the ball.

She reached up to make sure her mask still concealed her face. Her scalp itched from the red wig, but she dared not remove it. Anyone who had seen her at the masque would be hard-pressed to identify her, thanks to the disguise.

They reached the end of Delmont's property, and Robert and Ian slowed their mounts to a walk. She had hoped they would end up in Mayfair, where even at this time of night, it would appear improper for a lady to ride astride before a gentleman and she could make a quick escape. But to her dismay, they emerged into a quieter section of the city. The drizzling rain had stopped, and the night air was heavy with the scent of coal smoke. Modest town houses of red brick appeared ahead.

She turned in the saddle to glimpse at the man's profile. "Please let's part ways here."

"Not yet, but soon."

She thought he was heading for the town houses, but he turned down an alleyway leading back to the mews. The gas lamps that lit the main street illuminated nothing here, and she struggled to see in the dimness. No passersby were present, and her stomach churned with anxiety.

"Put me down now, or I'll scream," she demanded.

His lips were close to her cheek. "You're in no position to make demands, my lady. Not a sound or you'll alert Delmont's men or the night constables. Either could be close by."

She stilled. The truth of his words cut through her haze of panic. If she screamed, she could bring both the guards and the authorities bearing down on them. Neither were viable options. She had to take the risk that the man who called himself Robert would keep his word and release her. He had not harmed her tonight; rather, he had aided her in her escape from certain capture.

"And what about you?" she said.

"I don't plan on answering to either."

Who are you? The question asked itself again.

They entered the mews, and the scent of horses, hay, and dung permeated the space. She was not surprised to find that there were no stable boys to assist them at this time of night.

Ian dismounted and proceeded to take off the liveried footman's jacket.

Robert leaped down, then reached up to grasp her waist and help her to her feet. Bowing gallantly, he flashed a pearly smile, then raised her hand and brushed his lips across her fingers. "I never did learn your name," he murmured.

She was momentarily taken aback by his appealing smile and the brush of his lips against her flesh. Her relief that he was letting her go was slow to penetrate her senses. She felt the inexplicable pull of attraction testing her will. He had a coiled power, a captivating presence that hinted at forbidden excitement and temptation—certainly thoughts that a lady should never ponder. Yet, she longed to reach up and remove his mask, to see the whole of his features, how cheekbones, nose, and brow combined with the sensual lips and those piercing blue eyes.

Her voice was shakier than she would have liked. "My name is of no consequence, sir."

"*Ah,* even after our adventurous evening?"

"Especially after this evening."

No matter how charming he appeared, he was prying, still attempting to learn her identity. Thank heaven her mask and wig had remained in place during their flight. She doubted they would ever run into each other again. Although she had failed to obtain the documents she wanted from Viscount Delmont's library, her imminent freedom was what concerned her. She would find another way to incriminate the viscount.

He sighed as he loosened his cravat and pulled the silk free of his shirt points. "I do apologize, my mystery lady, but necessity requires it."

Too late, she realized his intent.

"No!" she cried out.

His hand snaked out, and he pulled her back to him. She struggled wildly, slamming her heel into his instep. He grunted, but his grasp didn't loosen, and he removed her mask and flung it aside. Covering her mouth with the cravat's snowy silk, his strong fingers worked a knot behind her head.

"What the devil—"

The red wig dropped to the straw at her feet. Night air tingled her scalp. She continued to struggle, but he was relentless as he worked the pins that held her hair in a knot atop her head. Chestnut tresses tumbled down her shoulders.

"Ah, that explains the eyes," he said in a low voice.

Unable to speak, she twisted in his arms and shot him a withering glance.

Ian handed Robert a short rope from the stable wall and he quickly bound her hands in front of her. He then retrieved the wig and stuffed it in his jacket pocket.

He turned to his accomplice. "I'll contact you once I've delivered the package," he told Ian.

"The marquess is going to want answers from her," Ian said.

Robert's voice was firm. "I'll get them."

A shiver ran down Sophia's spine.

Moments later, she found herself upon the horse with him mounted once again behind her. As he guided the horse farther down the alleyway, a cold knot fisted in her stomach. Why was he taking her with him? If he had stolen the "package" he was after, why did he not release her?

He pulled the horse up at the rear of one of the town houses. Lifting her down, he held her arm firmly as he guided her to the back servants' entrance.

Her brain was in tumult. Once he took her inside, she would be completely at his mercy. He could use any of the dastardly tactics Delmont was known for during interrogation. She struggled anew, kicking at his shins.

Never breaking his stride, he snatched her up like a piece of baggage and swept her over his shoulder. With one arm clamped about her thighs, he proceeded to the back door.

Before he knocked, the door opened to reveal a stern-faced butler with the look of a gunnery sergeant. He didn't even arch an eyebrow at the sight of a lady bound and gagged, dressed in full evening wear, and flung over a man's shoulder.

"The marquess is expecting me."

The butler opened the door wide. "Put your guest in the sitting room."

Robert strode inside. From her awkward angle she saw the slate tiles of a kitchen. The air was redolent with the aroma of roast lamb. Continuing through the kitchen, they turned left down a long hall and entered into a sitting room where he unceremoniously deposited her on a settee. Struggling to sit upright, she glared up at him. The butler lit two lamps and departed.

Robert crouched, and she found herself looking into the enigmatic blue of his eyes. Her first thought was that he had discarded his mask. Her second was that she had never seen a face as vividly handsome.

Bronzed skin stretched over high cheekbones and classically chiseled features. The dip in his chin was designed to make a woman want to press her lips there to see if he was truly flesh and blood or an artist's marble carving. A lock of his hair fell artfully across his forehead to brush straight brows in a style many dandies would surely envy.

But despite his handsome countenance she could see him for who he truly was—deceiving and unscrupulous.

She cringed as he pulled a knife from his boot, the lamplight flashing off the steel blade, but he merely cut her bindings and loosed the cravat tied behind her head. She swallowed hard and rubbed her wrists.

"My superior does not like surprises. I'll ask you again, who are you?" he said.

His superior? Good Lord, what had she gotten herself mixed up in?

"You first," she said. "And don't you dare tell me you were merely a guest at the ball. You had a well-organized escape plan tonight."

"I told you. My name is Robert." He reached out and traced her collarbone with his finger. His touch was gentle, catching her off guard. But before she knew it, he had her filigree chain wrapped around his finger. With a slight tug, the latch gave way.

"My locket!"

The necklace had been given to her by her father on her eighteenth birthday. He opened the heart-shaped locket, and read out loud, "To my darling Sophia. From Papa with love."

"You swine!" She tried to snatch it from his gasp, but he held it out of her reach.

He studied her intently, his stare bold as he assessed her disheveled chestnut hair, then her eyes before lingering at her mouth. "Sophia." He repeated her name as if testing the sound on his lips.

Then he stood, his fluid movements reminding her of a jungle cat. Reaching into his jacket pocket, he pulled out the red wig and tossed it into her lap.

His lips curled into a lazy smile. "You look better as a brunette, Sophia."

He strode to the door and closed it behind him, the distinctive sound of the bolt locking her inside reminding her of the gunshot that had torn through Delmont's library tonight.

She sprang to her feet, studying her surroundings for any means of escape. It was an elegantly furnished sitting room, of a type that could be found in any of the beau monde's town houses. Decorated in the Egyptian style, the windows were hung with blue silk drapes; a pair of chairs with sphinx feet was situated before a stone fireplace, a writing desk in the corner. Small brass replicas of the sphinx flanked an ormolu clock on the mantle. Attempts at opening the casements failed and she realized they had been deliberately sealed.

She returned to the settee and rested her head in her hands. She had been certain the potential reward of her actions justified the means tonight. She needed solid proof of Delmont's perfidy, and what better place to look than his own library. Her father had mentioned Delmont's safe.

Unbidden images of her father burned her memory, and

she swallowed back tears. In her mind's eye she saw him tinkering in his workshop, the table cluttered with steel pistons, mechanical parts, and shelves of jars containing labeled gases and liquids. She pictured him writing furiously in his ledgers, drawing diagrams of chemical formulas and inventions still in development, awaiting prototypes.

Her earliest childhood memories were of him inviting her into his workshop, discussing his latest inventions, grease beneath his fingernails as he pointed to rough sketches on the pages. His enthusiasm had ignited a similar passion within her, and she had spent hours alongside him, studying his experiments in the hopes of one day coming up with her own inventions.

But most recently, she recalled his troubled expression and deep frown lines between his brows when his work was deemed eccentric, not worthy of notice from the London Inventors' Society. He had been labeled the "Mad Marquess," and had become a figure of fun—the object of the *ton's* cruelty.

Sophia had been embarrassed. What a fool she'd been.

His inventions had been noted worthy by the Crown. The Society had stolen them from him, and then they had murdered him.

I failed you in life, Father. But If I escape this, I won't fail to avenge your death.

Chapter Four

Robert entered Wendover's study to find him seated behind his desk. Wendover removed his gold-rimmed reading glasses and looked up from the stack of papers he had been studying.

"I retrieved the package, but I ran into a complication," Robert said.

"By a complication, are you referring to the young lady locked in my sitting room?"

"I am."

"What else?"

"One of Delmont's guards was killed."

"Were you spotted?"

"No."

"Is she working for the Inventors' Society?"

"I don't believe so."

Wendover sighed and clasped his hands before him on the walnut surface of his desk.

Robert studied him. Everett Radley, the ninth Marquess of Wendover, had been Robert's superior at the Home Office for eight years. In his late forties, perhaps early fifties, he had a head of thick, graying black hair and a dark complexion more akin to a Spaniard than an Englishman. He was a quiet man and highly respected in society.

The *ton* did not know the true nature of his work, only that he maintained government offices in Whitehall and was privy to the secretary of the Home Office as well as the prime minister. It was common knowledge that he assisted the ordinance department and had been pivotal in supplying English troops with the munitions necessary to defeat Napoleon at Waterloo. Most of society assumed that he had no interest in marrying and was a reserved, brooding gentleman of duty. Only a hand-selected few knew of his covert workings.

Robert was one of them.

"Have you discerned the woman's identity?" Wendover asked.

"She refuses to speak. I thought to meet with you before I attempted any further interrogation." Robert placed the locket on the desk. "I believe her name is Sophia."

As soon as the marquess spotted the locket, he bounded out of his chair. "Sophia?"

"Does the locket or the name have significance?"

"I'll need to see her."

Wendover went to a painting on the far wall and lifted it down to reveal a small panel in the plaster. He slid the panel open to reveal a view of the adjoining sitting room. Robert knew the town house was not the earl's residence, but one of several working safe houses. The secret opening was visible only from the study into the sitting room and came in useful when Wendover desired to observe suspects who were brought here for questioning.

Wendover peeked into the sitting room, took a deep breath, then stepped back. "I'll be damned."

Robert masked his surprise. In all the years he had worked for the marquess, he had never seen a crack in Wendover's calm demeanor.

"I see you know the lady. Can you please enlighten me as to her identity and why she sneaked into Viscount Delmont's private library and held a pistol to my head?" Robert said.

The marquess slid the panel closed and returned to his desk. Robert followed and took his seat.

"Her name is Lady Sophia Merrill. She wasn't trying to kill you. It's Viscount Delmont she's after," Wendover said.

"Why?"

"Her father was the Marquess of Haverton."

"Haverton? The inventor?"

"One and the same."

As he had recently petitioned for membership into the London Inventors' Society, Robert knew all about Haverton. Others called the marquess eccentric; Robert called him a genius. The high-pressure steel pistons he had designed were being incorporated into the newly developed steam engines for trains. He was also a brilliant chemist and was rumored to have been working on a poisonous gas, completely indiscernible to human smell and taste.

"Haverton hasn't been seen publicly in some time," Robert said.

"That's because he was found murdered."

"Murdered? By whom?" Robert had known of two murders in the last six months; both were members of the

Society.

"We suspect Lord Delmont's involvement. Haverton's body was found in a brothel in St. Giles. The constable ruled it an overdose of opium. Due to the embarrassing circumstances behind the death, it has been kept quiet. Only his close friends and a few members of the Inventors' Society are aware of his passing, although not the gruesome details. But I do not believe the cause of death was an opium overdose," Wendover said.

"You have evidence of this?" Robert asked.

Wendover studied the crackling coals in the hearth. "I'd known Haverton since childhood, and we both grew up as elder sons and heirs of marquesses. He did not drink; he did not smoke. He was a recluse whose only interest was in his current invention. He had no desire to seek out prostitutes, let alone opium. His addiction was his work."

The marquess sighed and turned to Robert. "The evidence points to his being murdered and his body placed in the brothel afterward. Upon investigation by one of my agents, we discovered his home ransacked and his notes missing."

"Someone stole his latest inventions," Robert said.

"That's what we believe. His wife died twenty years ago, and he never remarried. His only living child is Lady Sophia."

Things were beginning to make sense to Robert. "She wants justice for her father's murder."

Wendover nodded. "She came to me a week ago, begging for my aid. She knows of my involvement with the ordinance department, but she doesn't know of my activities with the Home Office. She understood I was good friends with her father, and I told her the constables were doing everything in their power to find the responsible criminal."

"I take it she was impatient," Robert said.

"She had unearthed entries in one of her father's journals showing he suspected corruption in the Inventors' Society. Haverton had specifically mentioned Viscount Delmont."

"Did Haverton name others or give details on what type of corruption he suspected?"

"Unfortunately, he did not. But Haverton was certain Viscount Delmont was involved, and mentioned a bad falling-out between them, which resulted in Haverton's expulsion from the group. Sophia thinks her father was investigating the members—Viscount Delmont in particular—and that's why he was thrown out. She understands it takes a considerable amount of evidence to arrest a peer of the realm, and she asked me for help in pursuing Delmont."

"I assume you turned her down," Robert said.

"Of course. She doesn't know the Home Office is looking into both Delmont and the Inventors' Society. As her father's friend, I want to ensure her safety. I never thought she would plot and carry out such a disastrous scheme as to sneak into Lord Delmont's private library with a loaded pistol."

Robert thought of the wig and the mask. "She took care to hide her identity."

"Sophia was stubborn as a child and headstrong as a young lady, but I never believed she would take matters into her own hands."

"You cannot control other people's actions, my lord," Robert said.

"I can't help but feel responsible for her well-being." Wendover braced his arms against his chair. "Did you retrieve the documents from Delmont's safe?"

"Yes." Robert withdrew the ledger and packet from his jacket pocket and handed them over. "I haven't looked at them. I hope they hold the information we need."

"Delmont is working for someone," Wendover said. "A mastermind of the group. My theory is they are stealing specific types of inventions for profit. All of the works can be utilized by a militia. One of the victims invented an improvement to the double-barreled pistol, the other to the firing mechanism for cannons, and Haverton was a chemist working on a poisonous gas. We don't know exactly what they are planning or when they will make their move. There's even a possibility that government officials may be involved."

"They could sell the inventions to the highest bidder. England could suffer horrendous consequences," Robert said.

Wendover's brow furrowed. "It is not an investigation I take lightly. The mastermind will have to make contact with Delmont soon." He glanced at the stolen documents on his desk. "The ledger belonged to Haverton. The notes in the packet are in Viscount Delmont's handwriting. I hope they reveal names. Unfortunately, there is not much to go on except this." Opening his desk drawer, Wendover removed an object and rested it on the mahogany surface.

Robert reached for the gold gear and examined the tiny teeth and identifying stamp in its center. No bigger than an inch in circumference, the gear bore the mark of what appeared to be the capital letter *I*.

"What mechanical device is it from?"

Wendover shook his head. "None that I'm aware. It was found as a watch fob on two of the bodies."

"Engineers use gears, but this one is very small. The *I*

could stand for inventor. Could it be a commemorative token upon admission into the Society?"

Wendover shook his head. "I've spoken with a dozen members. None have received commemorative objects upon entry into the group."

"Where do you want me to start?" Robert asked.

"Delmont's hosting a house party at his country residence in Hatfield in two weeks. Numerous inventors are invited with their wives. Your petition for membership was a strategic decision to gain access to the group and assure you an invitation. I had planned on your attending along with Lady Marilyn. She was to distract the gentlemen and keep watch while you searched the place and discovered the truth behind the murders."

Robert was familiar with Lady Marilyn. The widow of a late baron, she occasionally aided Wendover with his investigations.

"I work alone, my lord."

"I'm afraid you must have a female partner for this affair. Delmont's wife is inviting only married or engaged couples. She plans on entertaining the women while Delmont meets with the men. I leaked word that as the new Earl of Kirkland you are soon to be betrothed."

"I see."

"But to my dismay, Lady Marilyn's mother is gravely ill and she refuses to leave her side."

"Then I'll go alone. Her absence will not hinder me from determining the contents of Delmont's numerous safes."

"Yes, but—"

Thwack.

A loud *thump* from the adjoining sitting room drew their attention. Wendover stood. "What the devil was that?"

"If I had to guess, I'd say our guest is destroying your

artifacts," Robert said.

"It's time to deal with Lady Sophia." Wendover retrieved his jacket from behind his desk chair and went to the door.

Robert moved to the hidden panel, slid it open, and glimpsed movement in the adjoining room. Lady Sophia clutched a small brass sphinx and paced the red carpet. Stopping by the door, she slammed the sphinx against the handle. When it refused to turn, she stomped her foot.

She has guts! It was admirable, if not wholeheartedly impetuous.

When he first saw her, he had suspected she was one of Delmont's spies, a consummate actress portraying an innocent miss. He'd been wrong; he could see it now. She was a lady driven to an incredibly reckless act. She could have been killed tonight, or worse, captured by Delmont's private guards.

The thought of what Delmont would have done to her beauty and spirit left a strange sinking in Robert's gut.

Sophia turned and looked toward the wall, directly where the panel lay hidden. Her green eyes widened as if she knew someone was watching her.

Green eyes just like Gwendolyn's.

Robert frowned at the thought. Countless women had green eyes, yet he'd never before compared another woman with Gwendolyn. As for what Gwendolyn and Sophia had in common: absolutely nothing. Gwendolyn was pure and innocent, without guile or daring. Completely unlike the impulsive, reckless woman before him.

So why was he thinking about his dead wife?

Robert shut the panel and stepped back.

• • •

Sophia jumped as the sitting room door swung open. Two men entered. Her gaze flew from the tall, tawny-haired man to the second shorter figure, and she gasped.

"My lord!" She ran to the marquess's side and grasped his hand. "Thank God you're here! This man"—her gaze moved to Robert—"this man abducted me and locked me in this room."

Wendover plucked the brass sphinx from her grasp and led her to a leather chair before the stone fireplace. "Sit, Sophia," he said, returning the artifact to its shelf and taking a seat across from her. "Lord Kirkland works for me, and he has advised me of tonight's events."

She took a quick breath of utter astonishment. She knew the name. It had been in the newspapers about six months ago. The old earl and his only son had died in a tragic carriage accident, leaving the nephew to inherit the title. She hesitated, blinking with bafflement. "Lord Kirkland…but this man's a thief—"

"Sophia, your behavior tonight was beyond careless," Wendover admonished.

She forced her gaze away from Lord Kirkland. Why would an earl work for the Marquess of Wendover? "I'm sorry for any inconvenience my actions may have caused, but—"

"Inconvenience! You could have been killed."

Her spine stiffened. "I asked you to help me."

"What makes you think I'm not doing all in my power to see justice done as concerns those that harmed your father?" Wendover asked. "I'm in constant contact with the constables. Lord Haverton was my close friend, and I feel obligated to look after your welfare. I promise we'll find the culprit."

"We know who the culprit is."

"What I mean to say is we lack the evidence to arrest a man of Lord Delmont's rank, but the constables are investigating every lead."

"Meanwhile my father's murderer roams free, hosting lavish masquerade balls. I can find the evidence needed better than any constable," she retorted.

Wendover's voice hardened. "Listen to me, Sophia. I want you to go home and stay there and let the authorities handle the investigation."

"I'm afraid I cannot."

The marquess leaned back in his chair, and she feared she had pushed him too far. He would throw her out of his house and into the street. Which made her wonder, why was he here in the first place? From what she recalled, the marquess lived in a mansion in Portman Square. Nothing about tonight made sense to her, certainly not the mysterious Lord Kirkland standing in the corner of the room glaring at her.

Wendover cleared his throat. "The truth is there is more at stake than just your father's murder."

"What do you mean?"

"There have been others, all inventors, brilliant minds who have been murdered."

"You suspect Viscount Delmont?" she asked.

"He is not solely responsible for the inner workings of the Inventors' Society," Wendover said.

"But he's the head of the group."

"Only as a figurehead for polite society."

"Then the members should be warned!" she insisted.

"We do not know who is involved and who is innocent."

She stared, her heart pounding. "You are more than just an ordinance officer, aren't you?"

"I am."

"Please, let me help."

Wendover remained silent for several heartbeats. "If I cannot have your cooperation, then I must have you watched." The marquess turned to Robert. "Delmont's house party."

Robert's eyes narrowed. "No."

Wendover continued. "Delmont is hosting a house party in Hatfield. Lord Kirkland is invited and as his betrothed you will accompany him."

Shock flew through her. "Betrothed!"

"I'm not a nanny," Robert growled.

Wendover glanced at Kirkland. "No, you're not. But you're the best I have. As Sophia seems bent on acting recklessly, I need a good man to ensure her safety. And you need a lady to accompany you."

"Must we put on such a drastic pretense as to be engaged?" she protested.

"You wanted to be involved, remember?" Wendover said. "It's the only way for you to attend."

"I don't want Lord Kirkland to watch over me," she insisted.

"It's the ideal opportunity. As the daughter of an inventor, you will have much in common with the wives. Viscount Delmont has no idea we suspect his involvement, and if you play your cards right, you will be able to convince him he is not a suspect in your father's murder. By your putting him at ease, Lord Kirkland will be able to conduct his investigation. You want to help, don't you?"

"Yes, but—"

"Those are my terms. Robert has work to do as an agent, and you will assist him by discreetly finding out as much information as possible from the wives. I'll have to arrange for the reading of the banns, however, you can cry off and end the 'engagement' when the investigation is over. It will cause a bit of a scandal, but it will pale in comparison to the arrest of Viscount Delmont. The gossips will be consumed with the daily excitement and drama of a trial of a peer."

"What about Lord Kirkland's…behavior?" she asked.

Robert chuckled and leveled his blue gaze on her. She returned the look without flinching.

"You need not worry about Lord Kirkland acting inappropriately," Wendover said. "He may have recently inherited an earldom, but he has been working for the Home Office for years. He is a consummate professional."

"He's a spy!"

He did not strike her as a spy who could infiltrate the Inventors' Society. Most of her father's friends and fellow members had been old, stern-faced men with complexions pasty from being cloistered in their laboratories.

"And what of my reputation?" she argued.

"I've thought of that. Your elder cousin, Lady Stanwell, is attending. She can act as your chaperone," Wendover said.

"Jane?" Sophia burst out, shocked. "But she's recently widowed."

"It's been over a year, my dear. She's a proper chaperone for you during the betrothal."

"Yes, but she's still grieving from…from her loss."

Of her husband's suicide. The thought died on Sophia's lips. At twenty-six years old, Jane was only two years Sophia's senior. They were friends, and Sophia knew her cousin suffered from her spouse's shocking betrayal.

"Lady Stanwell's husband was a member of the Inventors' Society, and Viscountess Delmont has invited her," Wendover said.

"Jane will not believe in a sham engagement," she retorted.

"Then you'll have to convince her, my dear."

How would she accomplish such a feat? Jane knew Sophia was hell-bent on pursuing justice for her father. Could she convince her cousin that she had somehow fallen madly in love with a man over the course of a month?

If she wanted to help find her father's killer, she'd have to. She glanced at the elusive Lord Kirkland leaning in the corner. He didn't look pleased by the notion and a sliver of feminine vanity took offense at his outward show of hostility. It nearly radiated from his pores.

Wendover had said she'd be safe with him.

Safe was the last word she'd use to describe him. She would have to be blind not to acknowledge he was a handsome man—the type of man women would do reckless things for. But his appearance wasn't what unsettled her. Rather it was the look in his glacial eyes, the tilt of his chin, and the confident, almost arrogant set of his shoulders.

Ruthless.

Wendover stood and went to the door. "I'll leave you two alone to discuss the arrangement."

Chapter Five

Robert pushed away from the wall and walked toward Sophia with loose-limbed grace. Stopping within a foot of where she perched on the edge of the settee, he glared down at her.

"I never work with a partner," he said.

She stood and raised her chin a notch. "Then who was the footman bearing Delmont's crest?"

"Ian was a necessity tonight, not a partner."

"That's illogical."

"Nothing about this situation is logical."

She took a deep breath. "It seems we don't have a choice in the matter. The marquess said we are to—"

"You're impulsive and reckless," he said coolly. "A danger to yourself and others."

Her temper flared. "And you're not? Breaking into Viscount Delmont's safe during a masquerade?"

"I'm highly trained, not a nanny."

She eyed him warily. "What exactly do you do for Lord

Wendover?"

Robert shrugged. "This and that."

"What on earth does that mean?"

"I'm skilled with safes."

"A safecracker?"

"Among other things."

"But you are an earl. However did you learn to crack safes?"

"I studied mathematics and engineering at Oxford."

She understood his background. By studying both engineering and mathematics, he had a solid understanding of basic physics and how things worked. For some reason, he'd chosen to apply his aptitude in a highly unorthodox way.

"But you remain working for the Home Office under Lord Wendover even after inheriting an earldom?"

"Yes."

He was a man of few words. She wanted answers, but he certainly was not forthright. "Other than leading a double life, a titled gentleman and member of the House of Lords by day and a spy in the evening, is there anything else you do that I should be aware of?"

"No."

Frustration roiled inside her. "If it's any consolation, I don't like the idea of working together any more than you do."

"I highly doubt it."

"It's true," she insisted.

"You appear quite eager to go along with Wendover's plans."

"I'm eager only to seek justice for my father's murder."

He hesitated, and his gaze roved and lazily appraised her. "You do realize we'll attend the house party next week as an engaged couple."

She felt her face grow warm, and she looked up at him with an effort. "In name only."

"It makes no difference. We'll have to socialize. Act as a loving couple. Sit beside each other during the evening meal and stare longingly into each other's eyes. It's not too late to change your mind."

"I won't."

He flashed a smile, his teeth white against the bronzed perfection of his face. "Perhaps we should practice to be certain we can pull it off."

He took a step closer and cupped her face with his hand. His palm was calloused, not as smooth as she would have expected of a lord's hands. But then again, he wasn't solely an earl.

He leaned close until she could see the specks of blue in his brilliant eyes. A strange fluttering began in the pit of her stomach as he lowered his head inch by inch until his breath fanned her lips. Her heart slammed against her ribs.

He's going to kiss me! She lost her nerve and jumped back just before his mouth touched hers.

Blue eyes sparkled with mocking humor. "Most ladies find me irresistible," he drawled.

She shot him a withering glance. "You flatter yourself, my lord. I'm not 'most ladies.'"

He arched an eyebrow, a spark of some indefinable emotion in his eyes. "True, but you should be warned that I'm a man who has a fondness for the opposite sex. I may succumb to my weakness while acting out our charade."

She swallowed hard—and to her dismay—her voice broke slightly. "You are the self-professed professional. You should exhibit control."

He shrugged a shoulder. "Even professionals experience desire."

She met his gaze without flinching. "It's a chance I'm willing to take."

...

"You look like you could use a drink."

Robert took the glass of whiskey Wendover held out to him. They were back in the earl's study, only this time Robert wasn't sitting before the large desk, but pacing the Oriental carpet. He felt caged and restless after his confrontation with Sophia.

He had purposely tried to intimidate her with a near kiss. He had hoped she would back down and change her mind about accompanying him to Delmont's house party. What he hadn't expected was the fire in her emerald eyes, the spark of excitement as his mouth came perilously close to hers. The fierceness of his own response had caught him off guard.

Lust had pounded in his head. Lust that was as dangerous as it was a despised weakness.

"Do not look so forlorn," Wendover said, leaning against a rosewood sideboard. "I had no choice. Lady Sophia must accompany you."

"So you keep insisting, my lord."

"I'm convinced of my decision."

"She's bound to get in my way."

"No, she won't."

Robert stopped pacing long enough to shoot the marquess

a hard glance. "How do you suggest I keep her from interfering, then? Do you want me to tie her to the bedpost each evening?"

The marquess sighed. "I don't expect you to involve her in your clandestine searches of Delmont's country house. Keep her busy talking with the wives. Perhaps she will learn something of use. Either way, the task will occupy her."

"And if it doesn't?"

"I trust you to use your discretion. Tell her enough to pacify her."

At Robert's silence, Wendover added, "You're the best I have, Robert."

He knew he was good. *Damn good.* If not for Sophia's interruption at the masquerade ball, he would have been in and out of Delmont's library well before the guards' rotation. He certainly wouldn't have had to shoot one of them or flee through the gardens.

He took a sip of whiskey and walked to a japanned curio cabinet in the corner of the study. He examined the artifacts—an eclectic assortment of painted Greek bowls, Arabic figurines, and African wood carvings, which displayed Wendover's exotic tastes.

"She's not a professional," Robert said. "She's bound to make a misstep, possibly put the mission in jeopardy. She doesn't trust me either. She looks at me like I'm a randy schoolboy ready to pounce upon her."

The marquess chortled. "We both know she's safe from you."

Ah, Robert mused. *But you don't know the extent of it, do you, Wendover?* After Gwendolyn's death Robert had sworn off women, not just emotional entanglements, but physical ones as well. His celibacy was a constant test of self-control.

He swirled the alcohol in his glass. Despite the fine quality of the aged whiskey, he felt oddly dissatisfied. It wasn't just the idea of marching into his next mission with Lady Sophia in tow. It was the cruel world in which he operated—the deception that was required of him.

When he had first drawn attention from the Home Office, he was finishing his last year at Oxford. As the nephew of the Earl of Kirkland, he had known he would have to make his own way in life. His family had paid for his education, and upon turning nineteen, he'd left Eton for Oxford to continue his studies. He'd done what young men did best: simultaneously pursue his academics and social life with equal exuberance.

After he'd started working for the Crown, he had felt a sense of patriotism. Never had he expected to meet and lose Gwendolyn or for his uncle and cousin to be killed in a carriage accident and for him to inherit the earldom. His work had always given him a true purpose in life. But now, years later, that initial altruism was gone, replaced with cold indifference.

Perhaps he had become too jaded or too cynical for the job.

Or, heaven help him, too old.

"One more?" Wendover asked, raising the decanter. Candlelight reflected off the cut crystal.

"No, thank you."

Wendover set the decanter aside. "You're acting a bit strange tonight."

"Any oddity in my behavior is from learning of my new partner."

"Is that all?" Wendover eyed him with a scrutiny that

had served him well over his years as a spymaster.

"Should there be more?"

"Do not be fooled, Robert. The mission might be a dangerous one. If Delmont or the ringleader, whoever he is, suspects you, then you will be in grave danger. You must have your wits about you."

Robert chuckled. "You need not lecture me, my lord."

The marquess's brows drew together. "Don't misunderstand. I'm merely concerned. We've been working together for years. If this is not a mission you wish to undertake, then I'll have to accept your decision."

Robert shook off his melancholy. "I have no qualms about the mission itself. Just the company."

...

The following morning, Sophia woke feeling anxious. After Wendover's footman had dropped her off at her home on Curzon Street late last night, she had been unable to sleep.

The memory of the evening haunted her. But rather than the shooting of Delmont's guard and their mad flight from the masquerade, it was the vivid images of Robert that kept her tossing and turning.

She relived the heat and strength of his body as he had pulled her to him seconds before the guard had burst into the library, the curve of his sensual lips as he grinned, the confident…dangerously graceful way he moved. And then there had been their private conversation later that night—the hammering of her heart as his large hand cupped her face and he lowered his head to kiss her.

Sophia pressed her hands to her heated cheeks. She

needed to clear her thoughts and prepare for the future, and there was only one place she could accomplish such a feat. Dressing in an old morning gown of blue cotton, she quickly scrawled a note for her cousin Jane and then headed for her father's workshop.

As a child, the workshop had reminded her of a mad scientist's lair, but as she grew older and her own inventive interests had been piqued, she looked at it as a haven.

A long wooden workbench ran the entire length of the back wall, its oak surface scarred and stained by the years. Tools, nails, oil pots, and iron parts were haphazardly strewn about it. On the opposite wall, rows of shelves held glass jars containing various chemicals of different colors; some were clear, others were blends of the color spectrum from yellow to green to bloodred. Sunlight streamed in through the windows, and the light reflected off the jars, creating a kaleidoscope of color on the wooden floorboards.

To those brave enough to visit the "Mad Marquess's" workshop, the room appeared unorganized and disorderly, but Haverton had known where every tool, mechanical part, and chemical was located. Sophia had taken over the workshop after his death. Her father's working habits had not been orderly, and to the dismay of the servants, she had inherited his traits.

She spread her father's notes across the workbench and began to combine chemicals into a glass beaker. Without his latest ledger, which detailed the gas he had been working on, she had struggled to replicate the formula.

Two hours later, a knock on the door startled her. The butler, Smith, stepped into the crowded room.

"Lady Stanwell is here to see you," he said. "She says it's

urgent—"

Before he could finish, a slender blonde woman burst into the room. "Sophia! I received your note. You said it was important."

Smith departed and discretely shut the door.

Sophia carefully set the beaker down and wiped her hands on a rag. Jane stood expectantly, dressed in the all-too-familiar, somber, black mourning gown.

"I'm glad you came, Jane," she said, "I have news. I'm engaged to be married."

Jane's mouth floundered open and closed. "What?"

"It's true."

"To whom?"

Sophia motioned for her to sit on the sole sofa in the workshop. Pushing aside additional papers, she sat beside her cousin.

"A gentleman by the name of Robert Ware," she said.

Jane's brown eyes widened. "The new Earl of Kirkland?"

First Wendover, now Jane. Did everyone know Kirkland?

"Yes, you know him?"

Jane's voice stilled. "Charles had admired a prized Arabian in Lord Kirkland's stables."

Sophia didn't miss the slight wince at the mention of Jane's deceased husband. Other than being the fifth Earl of Stanwell, Charles had been an aspiring inventor and a member of the Inventors' Society. He had dabbled with improving the axles used in carriages. Unlike Sophia's father, however, Charles's obsession had not been his work, but rather his addiction to betting on racehorses.

Sophia twisted her hands in her lap. "Yes…well…Lord Kirkland has proposed marriage and I've accepted."

"You never said a word," Jane said, not bothering to

hide the hurt in her voice. "I wasn't even aware he had been courting you."

Sophia stirred uneasily in her seat. "I've kept it to myself after Papa's passing." She knew she was making a mess of things. Even the man's name was still foreign to her and did not roll smoothly off her tongue.

Jane regarded her quizzically. "Yes, about that. I thought you were highly suspicious of the constable's findings surrounding your father's death. You believed your father was murdered. You swore to find the criminal and see justice done, remember?"

Sophia chose her words carefully. "I met Robert by chance at an outing, and he has been an unexpected source of comfort. As a new and influential earl, he agreed to help me with the constables and he has aided me in looking into Papa's death. Somewhere along the way, he has captured my heart."

God forgive me for lying, she prayed silently.

Jane clasped Sophia's hands, her eyes imploring. "Be careful, Sophia. The heart can be a dubious thing."

Sophia swallowed the lump in her throat. She knew her cousin continued to suffer over her husband's tragic death. Charles had shot himself with his own pistol after his prized stallion had lost an important race.

"I must beg a favor of you," she said. "I understand you are attending the Delmonts' house party in Hatfield in a fortnight at the viscountess's invitation. Lord Kirkland is attending as well and I'm invited as his betrothed."

"You need a chaperone?"

"Yes."

"I'm surprised. You had your suspicions about Viscount

Delmont. Why would you want to attend his weeklong house party?"

As Sophia's friend and cousin, Jane knew a few details about her investigation into Viscount Delmont. Sophia had never told her about her plans to sneak into the masquerade; she knew Jane would not have approved. And after last night, she understood that there was much more at stake than just her own father's death. Other inventors had been murdered, a mastermind of the Inventors' Society was suspected, and the Home Office was involved. Although she wanted desperately to confide in Jane, she was worried about her cousin's safety. The less Jane knew, the better.

"I…I admit I may have been wrong about the viscount," she said. "Delmont's interests lie in chemistry, and I fear I may have erroneously assumed he was after Father's work. The truth is Lord Kirkland and I have been unable to find anything incriminating about him."

"I see." Jane sighed. "Due to the excitement of your news, I forgot to mention what I learned. Lady Mason told me that there was a shooting last night at the Delmonts' masquerade. One of the viscount's guards was killed. Thieves are suspected."

"A thief?"

"No, *thieves*. They were spotted fleeing into the woods."

Sophia tried to still the pounding of her heart. "How awful! Were they caught?"

Jane shook her head. "No. The guards could not even identify the criminals for the constables. With footpads lurking in the streets and thieves breaking into mansions, London is becoming quite dangerous."

"Perhaps it's best if we leave town for a house party. Will you agree to act as my chaperone?" Sophia asked.

For a moment Jane studied her intently. "I will. I'd like to observe the two of you together. What better way to judge your newfound love?"

Sophia's stomach sank. She had no doubt the handsome and deceiving Kirkland could pull off the ruse. But could she?

Chapter Six

Later that afternoon, Sophia ceased working. She wasn't making any progress and her stomach was grumbling, reminding her she hadn't eaten luncheon. She was on the way to the kitchen when a knock sounded on the front door.

Smith had already opened it by the time she walked into the vestibule.

He held out a silver salver. "It's addressed to you, my lady."

Her name was written upon the envelope in bold black ink. She took the note and headed for the library. She broke the seal and tore it open to withdraw a sheet of heavy foolscap bearing the distinct watermark of one of London's quality papermakers.

> *Come to my home at three o'clock this afternoon. The party is less than two weeks away. We must prepare.*
> *Robert*

The missive was curt and lacked flowery prose, just like Kirkland. Sophia glanced at the mantle clock, her heart hammering. She looked down at her worn work gown and the smudges of dirt on her hands.

"Smith!" she called as she rushed out of the library. "Please summon the carriage. I must change and then attend to some business."

...

A half hour later, her carriage stopped before an impressive mansion in Grosvenor Square. Smoothing the skirts of her fine morning gown of blue alpaca, Sophia stared at the massive pile that had belonged to the old earl. Built of white stone with painted black shutters, the home's window boxes were bursting with well-tended, colorful blooms.

"Shall I accompany you, Lady Sophia?"

At the softly spoken question, Sophia glanced at her maid and chaperone seated inside the carriage. "Yes, Rose. But I shall require some time alone with Lord Kirkland."

Rose's eyes widened. "Is that wise, my lady? We're visiting a bachelor's home."

"We are discussing several of my father's inventions. It will take some time. Of course, you may stay if you deem it necessary."

Rose twisted her hands in her skirts, and Sophia knew she'd said the right thing. All her father's servants knew how tedious and long a conversation could be regarding one of his inventions, let alone several.

She'd once overheard the servants use the word "torturous"

when referring to her father's discussions.

"As you wish," Rose said, nodding obediently.

The driver hopped down to lower the step, and the women alighted the carriage. Together they headed for the front steps, and Sophia lifted the heavy brass knocker.

The door swung open and a dour-faced butler stared down at them.

"Lady Sophia Merrill to see Lord Kirkland. I believe he is expecting me."

The butler held the door open farther. The women stepped into the vestibule and handed him their cloaks. The entrance was stunning, graced by polished marble and a glittering chandelier.

"Lord Kirkland will see you in his study."

They followed him past an elegantly appointed drawing room, music conservatory, and dining room. The furnishings were rich mahogany, the carpets a lush Oriental, and the rooms spacious. Sophia marveled at Kirkland's wealth.

Her own father's town house on Curzon Street was in an affluent location, but he had never believed in luxury, and she had grown accustomed to living with a small staff. Her father had rarely entertained. Rather, he'd spent his money on his laboratory and his research.

The butler's heels clicked on the marble floor. His spine was rigid, the image of a perfectly proper butler in an earl's home. She couldn't help but wonder if the servants were aware of their new master's clandestine work for the Home Office.

A door farther down the hall opened and Kirkland emerged, carrying a sheaf of papers. His tawny hair was mussed as if he had repeatedly run his fingers through the thick locks. He wore no jacket, and the sleeves of his white shirt were rolled up, revealing his forearms.

He looked studious and reserved…completely different from the mysterious, masked man of last night, the dangerous spy who had snatched her off her feet and slung her over his shoulder like a pirate would his booty.

He glanced up from his papers and spotted her. His sensual lips curved in a smile. "Welcome."

Beneath his intense stare, a shiver of awareness tingled along her spine. "I received your note."

Kirkland turned to the butler. "Burke, I'd like to introduce my fiancée, Lady Sophia."

The butler stared, an expression of complete surprise on his face. Gathering his composure, he bowed. "Forgive me, my lady. I had no idea. It is a pleasure to meet you."

She curtsied. "Thank you."

"Perhaps Lady Sophia's maid would like refreshment in the kitchen," Kirkland prompted.

Burke was quick to catch on. "If you would accompany me, miss?" he said as he led Rose away.

Once they were alone, Robert ushered her into his study, closed the door, and motioned for her to sit in a chair before a pearwood desk.

Sophia sat and took in her surroundings. Several documents on the desk bore official seals, and she recognized them as letters patents granted by the Crown for new inventions. Engineering drawings and blueprints were pinned on a corkboard on the far wall. In the corner of the study stood a Pembroke table containing what could only be described as various innovations to inventions—a handlebar assembly of a velocipede, an electric battery, a miner's lamp, and good Lord, were those iron handcuffs?

"Thank you for coming." Kirkland sat in a leather chair behind the desk. "I see you find my collection of interest."

"Indeed," she said.

"I petitioned the Society for membership. I need to acclimate myself to the work of its members and offer a few of my own ideas."

"You thought of your own inventions?"

He smiled. "Don't look so surprised. I told you I studied engineering at Oxford."

She understood he would have to immerse himself in the group at the house party, feign interest in other's works, and be able to talk intelligently about his own inventive ideas. His background would surely aid him.

"I have something that belongs to you." Opening a desk drawer, he placed a battered, leather-bound book on the surface.

"My father's ledger! You did manage to steal it before I walked in on you in Viscount Delmont's library."

He merely chuckled.

"What else did you learn?" she asked.

"Wendover and I have both studied the ledger. Your father did not mention Lord Delmont or the Inventors' Society. The ledger contains numerous chemical formulas and documents his failed attempts at producing a poisonous gas indiscernible to human smell and taste."

She frowned. "Papa was a brilliant chemist. He wasn't attempting to produce a poisonous gas, but a harmless one that could be used by surgeons for their patients during surgery. But like many inventions, the object of father's initial work yielded unexpected results and an entirely different product."

"It's a loss he cannot finish his initial work."

"I hope to complete the formula."

"You are a chemist?"

"I am not as brilliant a chemist as my father, but I am not entirely ignorant either, and I hope to finish many of his mechanical inventions as well. His ledger will assist me."

"You are full of surprises, Sophia."

Was he complimenting her or criticizing her for dabbling in what many would deem a man's work?

"There's something else." He withdrew a small gold object from his pocket and placed it on the desk. "Do you recognize this?"

She picked it up and turned it over. "It's a gear," she said, frowning.

"Did your father own one?"

"He owned many gears. But none like this. Is it solid gold?"

"It is."

"Why is it significant?"

"It was found as a watch fob on the other bodies. I believe it has something to do with the murders. A sort of commemorative token upon admittance into the Society."

"To my knowledge, Papa never owned a small gold gear. What does it mean?"

"It's my job to find out."

"My father was a member until he was forced out by Viscount Delmont. I found entries in one of Father's journals where he suspected some type of corruption in the group. Soon after, he wrote that he had a heated argument with Delmont and was forced out, but he never gave specifics. I hope this information is useful to you."

"It is."

Kirkland leaned forward and rested his forearms on the desk. His tailored cotton shirt stretched tightly across his broad shoulders, emphasizing a sinewy strength. "The ledger is not the only reason I asked you here today. We need to think of our history."

"Our history?" she asked, bewildered.

"A believable story of how we met. Our love story."

Their love story? "Is that necessary?"

His voice held a distinct note of challenge. "It is if you refuse to stay home and out of trouble like Wendover had initially requested."

"I do."

His glance was bemused and opaque. "Then people will undoubtedly ask questions about us. I realize most unions are not love matches, but our situation must be different. Your parents are deceased, and you are of age. Wendover advised me that your father's estate was not entailed and that you do not imminently need to marry for financial reasons. Therefore, it will be much more convincing if we act the loving couple."

"I see," she murmured.

Glancing at his handsome visage, Sophia understood it would not be difficult for women to believe she had fallen head over heels in love with Lord Kirkland. To the contrary, it would be difficult to convince them otherwise.

"I spoke with my cousin, Jane, about our engagement," she said.

"Was her reaction that of disbelief?"

"She is my closest friend. I told her that we'd met by chance, and you were kind enough to assist me in looking into my father's death. I explained that over time we had fallen in love."

"Did she believe you?"

"I don't know. I'm not as accustomed to…" She trailed off. She wanted to say *lying,* but bit her tongue. "As accustomed to acting as you are."

A sparkle of humor lit his blue eyes. "Has Jane agreed to be your chaperone during the Delmont's house party?"

Sophia nodded.

"Good. I must thank your cousin before we depart. Until then, we'll have to contrive our love story and practice role playing."

A frisson of unease tingled up her spine. The last time he had wanted to "role play," he had come dangerously close to kissing her. She had lost her nerve and stepped away, but if she was truthful to herself, it was not out of fear of his kiss, but from her anticipated response.

"What exactly do you have in mind?" she asked hesitantly.

He stood and walked around the desk. "You look like a deer about to bolt from a hunter."

She rose and squared her shoulders at his comment. "Don't be ridiculous."

He came close and propped his hip against the desk. "Let's see. We first saw each other at a church service." He rubbed his chin between his thumb and forefinger. "No, that's too righteous. How about at a book-club meeting? Or a walk in Hyde Park?" He shook his head. "No, both are boring and lack spontaneity." Snapping his fingers, he caused her to blink. "I've got it! We met in Madame Beauxbaton's dance class."

"Dance class? But I know how to dance. No one will believe such nonsense," she protested.

"Yes, they will. Since your father's death, you've rarely attended balls or soirees. It's only natural to attend Madame's dance studio to brush up on your skills."

Her mouth fell open. He must have spoken with Wendover about much more than her financial independence. It was true she had been selective in which functions to attend and that was probably why she had never seen the new Earl Kirkland out and about in London.

After her father had been dubbed the "Mad Marquess," she had initially been ashamed, but then her anger had surfaced at the fickle members of the *ton*. She'd declined numerous invitations she'd received—no longer from embarrassment, but from fury. She understood herself enough to know that she would have defended her father and delivered scathing remarks to the hurtful gossips. Her impulsiveness and sense of righteousness would have demanded it.

At her stunned silence, he continued. "Both ladies and gentleman are seeking instruction due to the growing popularity of the waltz."

"The waltz? You can't be serious." Some considered the close proximity of the dancers scandalous.

"Don't be such a stickler. As I said, the waltz has become quite popular," he said.

She frowned. "What of Madame Beauxbaton herself? People will undoubtedly ask her about our so-called lessons," she pointed out.

He dismissed her concerns with a wave of his hand. "It's not a problem. She works for Wendover."

"Really? I would never have guessed."

"That's the point, my dear."

My dear. The endearment was improper, yet her pulse

quickened at the flattery nonetheless.

"It's the perfect story," Kirkland said. "It's quite romantic, don't you think, to meet during dance instruction? The women will be gushing over the tale."

The gossips would be in their glory. The daughter of the Mad Marquess had snared the most handsome bachelor in the realm while paying to learn how to dance the waltz. His appearance, combined with his title and wealth, had probably sent the debutantes and mamas of the *ton* into a frenzy.

His lips curled in a lazy smile. "The Camerons are hosting a ball tomorrow night. Wendover is friendly with Lady Cameron, and she has agreed to announce our engagement. You had planned to attend, correct?"

"Yes," she said hesitantly.

She had agreed to attend only because Lord Cameron had been an acquaintance of her father's. But now, the notion that her engagement would be publically announced made her highly uneasy. A hundred guests would attend the ball, all of them influential members of society.

Her chest tightened uncomfortably. It was one thing to tell her cousin she was engaged in the privacy of her workshop, but another entirely to have it announced in the Cameron's ballroom. There would be no going back; she was agreeing to a betrothal with Lord Kirkland, however long, to aid in investigating the Inventors' Society.

"Good," he said. "We will waltz at the ball and convince everyone of our story. Shall we practice?"

He stepped close and put a hand on her waist. Their eyes locked and her cheeks grew warm under the heat of his gaze. His shaving soap—a subtle scent of bay rum—teased her nostrils.

"We cannot," she blurted out. "There's no music."

He captured her right hand in his. "No matter. We're just practicing, remember? Put your left hand on my shoulder and follow my lead."

Sophia slowly raised her arm, and her fingers grazed his shoulder. The heat from his body seared her fingertips through the cotton shirt. Her pulse skittered alarmingly.

He began to move, smooth and practiced. "That's it, Sophia. One and two and turn…you have the basic steps. Excellent."

Only it was far from excellent. She was highly conscious of his hand at her waist, his sinewy body inches from hers. A tingling began in the pit of her stomach at his nearness. She stumbled; he steadied her.

Kirkland looked down, his stare bold as he assessed her. "The ball will be a good test to see how well you can handle the deception."

"I assure you, I can handle anything."

"Anything?" He pulled her a fraction of an inch closer.

His touch upset her balance, and she inhaled sharply. He was purposefully trying to unnerve her. "Deception comes that easy to you?"

"It's a requirement of my job."

"I must keep that in mind when dealing with you, my lord."

He stopped dancing, but his hand remained around her waist. "We are entering the enemy's lair. I need to be certain you won't panic."

Her chin rose a notch. "I never panic."

His voice was cold and exact. "Dispassionate control is required, or else dangerous mistakes can occur."

"If you're trying to intimidate me into backing out of Delmont's house party, then you're failing. I have mettle, my lord. Your seductive tactics won't work on me."

He arched an eyebrow. "What do you know of seduction?"

"I'm not completely ignorant. I'm twenty-four years old, and despite what you've heard, I've attended numerous balls, danced with plenty of gentlemen, and strolled through moonlit mazes. I've been kissed before."

Ocean-blue eyes studied her mouth. "Where?"

She frowned. "My lips and even once on my neck." She pointed to a spot just beneath her chin.

His gaze dropped to where her finger pointed, then slowly lowered to the skin just above her bodice. Her pulse skittered.

"Then you won't mind if I test your mettle?"

She stood frozen.

Looking into her eyes once again, he came close, moving slowly. He mouth brushed across hers, once, twice, a featherweight touch before she stepped back. Her fingers flew up to cover her lips.

"Just as I thought," he drawled. "You lack experience. A few stolen kisses inside a dim maze are not sufficient."

She bristled with indignation. "Not sufficient? Whatever else do you have in mind?"

"This." Pulling her close, he swooped down and kissed her.

His lips were full and warm, teasing hers. His tongue ran over her bottom lip with tantalizing persuasion, and she gasped. He took advantage of her parted lips to slide his tongue into her mouth. He tightened his hold, and her breasts pressed against his solid chest.

Sweet heaven! He was right; her prior experiences fell

far short when compared to the feel and taste of him.

Despite her prior misgivings, her instinctive response to his kiss was powerful. Her skin grew hot; her heart pounded an erratic rhythm. Her fingers rose of their own volition and trailed up his forearms. She felt the sprinkling of hair, touched the soft cotton of his rolled-up shirtsleeves, then moved higher to grasp his broad shoulders. His muscles were hard slabs beneath his shirt. Arching her body into his, a low growl rumbled in his chest. Encouraged, her tongue grazed his, tentative at first, until shivers of delight raced down her spine, and she returned his kiss.

Lifting his lips from hers, he trailed kisses down her throat, past the spot she had initially pointed to below her chin. Then his lips seared a path above her bodice and the overwhelming heat spread…flooding her limbs and pooling low in her belly.

It was everything she had ever dreamed a kiss would be and more. So much more.

She moaned low in her throat, winding her fingers around his neck and trying to cajole his lips back to hers.

He stiffened and pulled back, a frown marring his brow as he gazed upon her upturned face.

She ignored the strange aching in her limbs and tried to calm her pounding heart. To her dismay, he did not appear the least affected by the kiss.

He does this all the time, she thought. W*omen must throw themselves at him!*

Then she looked into his eyes and changed her mind. There was a wild darkness in the blue depths, a hint of tightly reined lust that was startling in its intensity.

"Did I pass your test?" she asked.

"I believe I had mentioned *dispassionate control.*"

She stiffened, momentarily abashed. "Despite your newly acquired title, you are not a gentleman."

"I wouldn't be successful if I were."

She took a step back from his towering frame. "I may be impulsive, but you are quite arrogant, my lord."

"Do not judge me too harshly, Sophia. You may think my tactics ungentlemanly, but my past results are unquestionable. I will find who is responsible for your father's murder and unravel the mystery behind the Inventors' Society."

She couldn't ask for more, could she? Still, she was having difficulty settling her racing heart.

Kirkland reached into his pocket and placed a flash of gold in the palm of her hand. "I believe this belongs to you."

She glanced down. "My locket!"

"I had the latch repaired. I apologize for my barbaric methods."

"Thank you, my lord."

"It's Robert."

She met his gaze. "I don't think that's proper, my lord."

"The world will soon think us engaged."

"Still, I don't think—"

"In private, then. The title is new to me and we are to work together, correct?"

A flutter of nerves swam low in her belly. "All right, Robert."

He handed her the ledger. "This is yours as well."

Her father's leather-bound book felt heavy in her hands. "Thank you for returning it, my lord…Robert."

"That's it." He walked her to the door and raised her hand to his lips. "Until the Camerons' ball tomorrow night."

Her treacherous body tingled from the contact, and she nervously bit her bottom lip.

"Are you sure you can carry this off, Sophia?" he asked.

"Yes." *No!* She wasn't certain of her resolve around him.

"What about your story?" she retorted. "What will you tell your friends and acquaintances about me?"

"Leave them to me."

Chapter Seven

Robert looked up from his brandy as his old-school friends, Gareth Ramsey and Daniel Forster, joined him at his table in White's club.

"It must be important news indeed for you to ask us to meet before noon," Daniel said, as a waiter arrived at their table and set down two additional glasses of brandy.

Gareth reached for his glass. "Now does this have anything to do with your tedious work for the ordinance department? You have a title now, you don't need to work in order to keep up appearances."

Robert leaned back in his chair. He'd been first to be recruited by the Home Office for his unique talents of finessing safes open. Thereafter Wendover had need of more agents—gentlemen who had access to high society and the *beau monde*—and Daniel and Gareth had been recruited. The three were no longer just former school friends; they were colleagues in espionage and akin to brothers.

"No, it has nothing to do with my work for the ordinance department. And I've told you before, I remain there because I enjoy it," Robert said.

"Does it concern your inheritance then? Don't tell me debt collectors are pounding on your door. Those parasites crawl out of the woodwork whenever someone unexpected inherits," Gareth said.

Robert chuckled. "No, it's not that either, but an important matter nonetheless."

Several tables away, an excited shout drew Robert's attention. A group of gentleman were playing a high stakes game of whist, a small fortune in banknotes resting on the table between them. The aristocracy and how easily they spent their money had always amused Robert. He was still unaccustomed to his new title and the additional wealth that accompanied it.

"Well, man, what could be so important?" Daniel asked, drawing Robert's attention back to them.

"I'm engaged to be married," Robert said.

Gareth and Daniel froze, both cradling their glasses, incredulous expressions on their faces.

"Aren't you going to wish me future happiness?" Robert said drily.

"We would if it made any sense," Daniel said.

"Who is she?" Gareth demanded.

"Lady Sophia Merrill, the daughter of the late Marquess of Haverton."

"Haverton? The Mad Marquess?" Gareth asked.

"I hadn't heard he died," Daniel said.

"It's been kept quiet by the family," Robert said.

"We didn't even know you'd been courting her. Come

to think of it, we didn't know you'd been interested in *any* woman lately," Gareth said mockingly.

Robert expected Gareth's sarcasm. After all, Robert had always enjoyed female companionship as a university student and years thereafter. His friends would often jest that they would wait by the wayside to console the barmaids Robert would reject. But circumstances had changed, and much to his friends' vexation, Robert had been celibate for the past two years.

Robert lowered his voice. "I've been assigned a new mission and Wendover insists that I need a lady to accompany me." He knew they wouldn't ask about the investigation. The Home Office demanded complete secrecy, and as spies themselves, they understood this rule. But that didn't mean they wouldn't inquire about Sophia.

"And you agreed to the engagement?" Daniel asked.

"The marquess believes it necessary," Robert said.

Gareth smirked. "She must be attractive."

Robert shot Gareth a black, layered look. "What makes you assume that?"

"You would never have agreed otherwise," Gareth said.

"I told you Wendover was insistent," Robert said tersely.

Gareth gave him a disparaging look that suggested he didn't believe a word that came out of Robert's mouth. "There's hope for you still."

Robert knew his friends mistook his current celibacy for lack of interest in women when the truth was it was a form of penance for a guilty conscience and a mission gone horribly awry.

A mission that had resulted in Gwendolyn's death.

"If either of you are asked, Lady Sophia and I met in

dance class," Robert said.

Gareth laughed. "Damn, Robert. If I'd known you had decided to return to enjoying bachelorhood and the ladies, I would have suggested a few establishments."

"I never had an interest in brothels," Robert said wryly. He knew Gareth would be the more difficult of his two friends. As a barrister who exclusively handled matrimonial matters, specifically legal separation, Gareth's attitude toward love and marriage was cynical and jaded.

Gareth waved him off. "Why not enjoy what life has to offer. Why agree to an engagement, even a convenient one?"

Daniel shot Gareth a hard stare. "Leave him be, Gareth. He's doing it for King and Country. Besides, matrimony does not have to be interpreted as a legal prison."

"Never mind you, Daniel," Gareth snapped. "Women have always been drawn to you. As the heir of a viscount, you have the pick of the litter."

"Your concern is noted, Gareth," Robert said. "But I assure you that the engagement will be terminated after the mission is completed. I know what I'm doing."

"Like hell you do," Gareth said. "You could easily get trapped into marriage. Don't come whining to me after the honeymoon is over. Even I can't undo it."

Daniel slapped Robert heartily on the back. "Don't listen to him, Robert. I'm relieved you've agreed to Wendover's demands, even if they are for appearances only. It tells me you've moved on after Gwendolyn."

Robert took a swallow of brandy. Both Daniel and Gareth knew Robert had been enamored of Gwendolyn, but soon afterward she had died and he'd told them she was killed in a riding accident. He couldn't admit the horrific truth behind her death, even to his close friends. Only Daniel knew how serious he had been about Gwendolyn or that they'd traveled to Scotland to marry.

But Robert had never told Gareth.

"I'd like to meet the lady myself. See what type of loveliness has finally pulled my friend out of celibacy," Gareth said, his words loaded with ridicule.

Robert studied his hawk-like features. "I'm certain you'll find her quite charming."

He'd have to warn Sophia about Gareth. He knew his friend had good intentions, but Gareth had little tact. As for his friend's legal services, thankfully Robert wouldn't need them. He had no intention of turning the betrothal into a real marriage.

. . .

After departing White's, Robert returned home, closed his study door, and slid the bolt in place. Behind his desk was a stone fireplace ready to be lit. Walking to the fireplace, he pressed the base of a silver candlestick resting upon the mantle and a stone loosened in the brickwork. He removed the stone to reveal a hidden safe.

Inside were a sealed envelope and a miniature portrait.

He reached for the envelope and returned to his desk. After breaking the seal, he withdrew a detailed map. Unlike most maps, this one did not show the distinguishing lines of passable roads, lakes, and hills, but revealed the detailed layout of the interior of Viscount Delmont's country manor in Hatfield. Neat block print identified each room, right down to the location of the furnishings and area rugs. Robert's eye was drawn to the small black questions marks in random rooms, noting where safes might be located.

His lips twitched. The marquess must have had an agent inside, most likely posing as Delmont's servant, who had drawn the map. He wondered if the agent had been Ian and what guise he'd donned. A footman again? Or perhaps a stable groom or manservant?

Ian was proficient, but Robert knew the question marks were just what they symbolized—guesses as to where the safes were hidden.

He would have to locate them on his own and find the best method of nondestructive manipulation. This time he wouldn't remove the contents, only study them for clues. If all went as planned, Delmont would never know that the safes had been tampered with or their contents investigated.

Carefully he folded the map and returned it to the safe. His hand hovered above the miniature portrait before removing the small gilt frame. Pain and loneliness squeezed his heart as he studied the image. Even now, years later, each time he envisioned Gwendolyn's death a primitive grief assailed him.

Her smile was just as he recalled, wisps of white-blond hair framing her heart-shaped face. She had been innocent, untainted by the evil and darkness that shrouded him. The talented artist had captured her green eyes perfectly...

He frowned. The image blurred before him, and he pictured another pair of green eyes. They radiated defiance and determination in their mesmerizing depths rather than sweet innocence. The hair was wrong...thick chestnut tresses tumbling in disarray...the lips full and sensual...the complexion not a pale hue, but a golden color that hinted at sunshine and brazenness.

Sophia.

When he had sent the note asking her to come to his home, he had planned on testing her...on dissuading her from the ridiculous notion that they could work together. He had waltzed with her, had kissed her, for Christ's sake, in an attempt to make her run from him straight to Wendover and cry off. But his plan had backfired.

As soon as their lips had touched, she had been as passionate and responsive as an inferno. He recalled the lush ripeness of her body pressing against his, of the tentative stroke of her hot tongue meeting his, and of her green eyes shimmering in burgeoning sexual awareness.

His response had been instant and combustible; he'd had to use every ounce of discipline to break the kiss and rein in his lust.

His fingers clenched the portrait. Damnation. Why was he thinking of Sophia? It was the first time he had looked upon Gwendolyn's portrait and thought of another woman. Guilt made his gut clench tight.

He refused to betray Gwendolyn's memory in such a fashion.

Returning the portrait to the safe, he shut the door and put the stone back in place.

Chapter Eight

"I hadn't expected this many people," Sophia whispered to Jane behind her fan in the corner of the Camerons' ballroom.

"There's still time to change your mind," Jane said. "Lady Cameron has not yet announced your engagement."

Sophia frowned at the hint of eagerness in her cousin's voice. "It's not my upcoming engagement that has made me uneasy, just the crowd."

The room was packed with well over one hundred guests. Women paraded about in ball gowns of every color of the rainbow—from demure pastels to bright jewel tones. The gentlemen were not to be outdone, and Sophia observed a mix of austere grays beside painted popinjays dressed in flamboyant-colored coats with striped and checked waistcoats and intricately folded cravats.

She glanced longingly at the open French doors leading out to the terrace. She hoped a breeze would cool her overheated skin, but to no avail. The air was heavy with the scent of costly French perfume and well-dressed, perspiring bodies.

She smoothed the skirts of her emerald gown. She had taken great care with her appearance tonight, and she knew the gown's color enhanced the vivid green of her eyes. The bodice was fashionably low, and an emerald necklace rested between her breasts. Matching emerald combs swept the sides of her chestnut hair away from her face, and loose curls fell down her back.

Jane looked lovely in a violet gown with her blond tresses artfully arranged atop her head. Over a year had passed since Charles's death, and Sophia was relieved that Jane had not worn one of the black mourning gowns that dominated her wardrobe.

The orchestra began a lively, Scottish reel, and men and women whirled on the parquet dance floor. Glasses clinked, voices soared, and jewels glittered.

Every few minutes Sophia glanced at the liveried master of ceremonies stationed beside the gilt banisters at the top of the ballroom stairs. His chest puffed with self-importance as his imposing voice announced the names of arriving guests.

Robert had yet to arrive. After two glasses of punch from the refreshment table, she'd begun to wonder if he would come at all. Then a prickle of awareness tingled down her spine, and she looked up and caught sight of him at the top of the stairs. Dressed in simple black-and-white evening attire, he looked magnificent, like a golden Adonis. A taller, dark-haired man stood beside him.

"Robert Ware, the sixth Earl of Kirkland. And Mr. Gareth Ramsey," the servant said in a booming voice.

Sophia recognized the name of the second man as one

of Baron Suffolk's sons and assumed he was friends with Kirkland.

A hushed murmur pervaded the ballroom as the women whispered behind fluttering fans and Lord Kirkland descended the stairs with smooth grace.

"Oh, my," Jane whispered beside her. "He's stunning."

Sophia turned to her cousin. "You said you knew him."

"I said I knew *of* him. I never met the man in person. His appearance is not a detail Charles would have passed along," Jane said.

Sophia seized the opportunity to convince Jane that the engagement was indeed real. "Can you understand why I am enamored of Lord Kirkland?"

Jane's dark eyes sharpened. "I never pegged you as the type of female to be taken in by a handsome face."

Sophia's voice was laced with frustration. "You mean as you were with Charles."

The color drained from Jane's face, and Sophia immediately regretted her careless words. "Forgive me, I—"

"You're right," Jane said. "I should not pass judgment. I haven't even met him." She studied the two men as they greeted their hosts, the Earl and Countess of Cameron. "I haven't seen Mr. Ramsey at a society function in years. The gossips said that he had a falling out with his father, Baron Suffolk. Is he friends with Lord Kirkland?"

Sophia glanced at the second man. Gareth Ramsey also wore black-and-white evening wear, but unlike Robert's stunning features, he had the rugged look of an unfinished sculpture. Robert was tall, but Mr. Ramsey was even taller. His broad shoulders, craggy face, and solid stance gave him the appearance of a seasoned boxer.

She could only presume the two men were friends since they had arrived together. "I believe Mr. Ramsey is in attendance tonight to support Lord Kirkland."

Robert and Mr. Ramsey made their way through the ballroom where they reached a group of men who detained them. Among the gentlemen, Robert stood out—not just for his looks, but for his commanding manner and confidence, as if he was unperturbed by the society ladies staring at him.

Sophia watched fascinated as he threw back his head and laughed at something one of his friends said. White teeth flashed in his bronzed face, and her heart thudded. He truly was spectacularly handsome. His ocean-blue eyes, chiseled nose, and the cleft in his chin would draw the attention of any female.

She recalled their shared kiss in his chambers, and her gloved fingers brushed her lips in wicked remembrance.

Just then he looked past his acquaintances and scanned the ballroom. Their eyes met, and his lips curled in a sensual smile.

Her breath hitched.

He spoke to his friend, and they excused themselves and made their way over to Sophia and Jane. Robert's gaze swept Sophia from head to toe, and he bowed. "You look lovely this evening, Lady Sophia."

"Thank you, my lord." A deeply buried part of her was thrilled he had noticed.

He turned to Jane. "I presume this is your cousin, Lady Stanwell."

Jane curtsied.

"My gratitude for your services as Sophia's chaperone for the upcoming house party," he said. "Your cousin means the world to me, and I would never do anything to make her feel uncomfortable."

The double meaning of his words was not lost on Sophia. If she didn't want to go through with their ruse, she had only to say the word.

Oh, he is as cunning as he is charming, Sophia thought.

Robert motioned to Gareth. "May I introduce a friend, Mr. Gareth Ramsey."

Gareth bowed. "A pleasure, ladies." Dark obsidian eyes traveled over Sophia to rest upon Jane.

Jane stiffened at his heated stare.

"Are you ready, Sophia?" Robert asked. "Lady Cameron is eager to make an announcement before the supper room is opened."

He offered her his arm and Sophia placed her gloved fingers on his sleeve. Nervousness gripped her. Unexpected as this engagement was, she couldn't back down. Not now… not when her goal was so closely within reach. With the Home Office investigating the case, her father's murderer would not go unpunished.

Robert led her to where Lord and Lady Cameron waited. The earl had a sparse head of hair, pleasant features, and twinkling blue eyes. The countess was a tiny woman, with an abundance of once auburn curls now fading gently to gray.

"You will make a handsome couple," she said.

Sophia smiled. "Thank you, my lady."

The older woman leaned close and lowered her voice. "Lord Cameron and I were saddened to learn of your father's passing. Haverton was a dear friend and a brilliant man. Society can go to the devil; there was nothing 'mad' about him."

Sophia's throat tightened at the kind words.

Lady Cameron clasped Sophia's hand. "Most believe Haverton is out of town on business. As close friends of the family, it's acceptable for us to announce the engagement. Are you ready, my dear?"

Sophia gave a curt nod. "Yes."

The countess waited for the last dance to end before clapping her hands and drawing the attention of her guests. "It is my pleasure to announce the engagement of Lady Sophia Merrill and Lord Kirkland."

There was an awkward silence as the guests digested the news that the daughter of the Mad Marquess was to marry an earl. Then Lady Cameron kissed Sophia on both cheeks, and Lord Cameron embraced Robert and slapped him on the back.

Circulating the ballroom, a dozen footmen carried trays of bubbling champagne, and the guests toasted their future happiness. Members of the *haute ton* approached to offer their congratulations.

Robert shook outstretched hands with a cool smile, and Sophia marveled at how easily he slipped into the role of engaged gentleman.

Just what situation would unnerve him? she wondered.

Lady Cameron motioned to the conductor and the orchestra struck up a waltz.

"Come, Sophia," Robert said.

He led her to the dance floor and placed his hand at her waist. As if in a trance, she put her hand in his and rested her fingertips on his shoulder. They stood so close their bodies almost brushed. Aware of every eye upon them, her heart beat so loudly she feared she would faint.

"Smile, Sophia. You wanted this, remember?"

Forcing her chin up, she met his eyes. "I won't back down."

"I never thought you would."

He swept her into the dance. Her stomach was in knots, but he was a marvelous dancer and as he whirled her around the floor she felt like she was drifting on a cloud. Her heart continued to pound—no longer from fear—but from excitement. The dance, the music, the man…all were thrilling. For a woman who had spent the past six months sequestered in her father's workshop, grieving the loss of her parent and obsessed with obtaining justice for his murder, dancing with him was exhilarating. She tilted her face up and found him watching her with an intent expression.

For a brief moment she imagined them truly engaged and a shiver rippled down her spine.

Stop this nonsense, Sophia! Such an attraction is perilous!

She reminded herself that they were playing a role. Deception was what he did best, what he was paid to do for King and Country. She'd be a fool to lose her heart and fall victim to a man like him.

Chapter Nine

The morning of their journey to the Delmont's house party arrived a fortnight later. Sophia followed two footmen as they carried her valises outside her town house and set them upon the steps. Jane had arrived earlier and was waiting beside her own baggage.

"He's coming," Jane said, drawing Sophia's attention to the street. A magnificent coach bearing the Kirkland crest with matching bays pulled up before them.

The door opened and Robert stepped down. Dressed in a deep blue coat that matched the exact shade of his eyes and form-hugging trousers, he looked striking. His fair hair was combed in the *à la Brutus* style currently popular with the dandies of the *ton*, but Sophia wasn't fooled. Robert Ware wasn't a fop, but a cunning spy.

He smiled charmingly. "Good morning, ladies. Are you prepared for our journey?"

With Jane acting as their chaperone, they would travel

to the Delmont's country property in Hatfield, twenty miles north of London.

"We're ready, my lord," Sophia said.

He nodded and turned to oversee the loading of the baggage, until Jane's voice halted him.

"Is Mr. Ramsey attending the house party?" she asked.

Robert arched an eyebrow. "Not that I'm aware, Lady Stanwell. Why do you ask?"

She shrugged. "You are friends and I assumed he had petitioned for membership as well."

"While we are school friends, I studied engineering and have an interest in inventing. Gareth, on the other hand, became a barrister whose interests and legal practice focuses on…on other matters."

Jane's lips parted as if to ask Robert to elaborate, but then she nodded, apparently satisfied with his answer, and turned away.

Sophia waited until he resumed his task with the baggage before drawing Jane aside. "What was that about?" she whispered.

"Nothing," Jane said.

"It sounded very much like something to me."

"Don't concern yourself, Sophia. As a newly engaged woman, you should be thinking only of Lord Kirkland."

Sophia felt her face grow warm. "I hope the upcoming week will allay your concerns about us."

"Meaning?"

"You need not watch us like a hawk," she said.

"That's my job as your chaperone."

Sophia clasped her hand. "Please don't worry so much. I want you to enjoy yourself as well."

Robert came over and opened the carriage door. Holding

out a hand, he assisted the women into the coach and settled himself on the bench across from them. His knees brushed Sophia's skirts, and a tingle of awareness crept down her spine. He was a tall man with broad shoulders—a too-big, too-lithe male whose presence seemed to fill every square inch of the vehicle.

The driver whistled. The coach lurched forward with a jingle of harness, and the bays set off at a brisk pace through the city streets.

They engaged in polite conversation to pass the time, and after an hour there was a lull.

Robert stifled a yawn. "Traveling always makes me tired," he said. "If you ladies will excuse me, I'd like to take a brief nap."

"Of course," Jane said.

He leaned back, shut his eyes, and folded his hands in his lap. Minutes later, he appeared to be sleeping, but Sophia wasn't convinced. There was a coiled tension in his sinewy frame that hinted of alertness.

Jane continued to talk and attempted to pick topics that she believed would interest Sophia, but Sophia found herself distracted. She continually stole glimpses at Robert, and more than once she stirred uneasily on her seat.

The problem was that despite her assurances to him, she had not conquered her misgivings about working together. She wondered just what her assignment would entail. Wendover had told her to speak with the wives in order to glean useful information. He understood that as the daughter of an inventor, she would be able to relate to the women. Her father had exhibited what many members of society considered eccentric behavior, and she knew he was not alone when it came to his endeavors. Most inventors were deemed peculiar by outsiders.

As for Robert, she pondered how often she would see him over the course of the week. Propriety dictated that Jane accompany them at all times. No one knew better than Sophia that Jane was observant and intelligent. Then how was she to pass along any useful information to him? Come to think of it, how was she to question the wives without arousing Jane's suspicions?

The scenery outside the window changed from crowded city streets to rural farmland, and the coach jostled across isolated country roads. Hours later, they stopped at a posting inn for the night. Robert made himself scarce in the taproom, and Sophia and Jane shared a repast of hot roast beef, boiled potatoes, and tea in a private parlor before retiring for the evening.

They resumed traveling early the following morning, and Sophia spent the remainder of the journey thinking of Viscount Delmont and how badly she wanted the blackguard to pay for his sins. She recalled how shattered her father had been after being evicted from the Inventors' Society. She imagined the physical pain he must have suffered the night he was murdered. He had been dosed with opium. Had he been alert and aware?

Had he cried out for her in his last moments?

Her hands clenched her skirts. She turned to Jane, but her cousin had stopped trying to engage her in polite conversation. Jane's head lolled against the side of the coach, and she dozed.

At last, the coach came to a long, winding drive lined with towering oak and spruce trees. Sophia woke Jane, and they looked out the window at Delmont's vast property. The grounds were meticulously kept with boxwood hedges, a large herb garden, and rose bushes, which filled the air with their sweet fragrance. A small orchard of peach trees, their boughs bursting with flowers that would soon bear heavy fruit, dotted the perimeter.

Sophia gasped as the country manor came into view. With white stone walls and four miniature crenellated turrets, it looked like a small castle from a fairy tale. Sunlight glimmered off a lake with a working fountain.

"It's lovely," Jane said.

Sophia stilled. The manor was beautiful, but it housed the enemy. Her unease increased as the carriage wound closer to the manor home. Now that she was minutes away from seeing Viscount Delmont in the flesh, could she go through with their plans? She wanted this, she told herself. She wanted to help catch her father's killer.

But unlike Robert, she was not a professional spy, trained to disguise her rioting emotions.

The carriage rounded the circular drive and halted by the front door. Her heart pounded.

I can do this! She had to find the courage to face the viscount. He'd probably be occupied with his fellow inventors during the week and pay the women little or no attention.

A strapping footman came down the granite steps and opened the carriage door. Robert stepped down and helped Jane and Sophia alight. The baggage was unloaded and the guests ushered into the house where a butler took their cloaks.

A crystal chandelier holding dozens of candles hung in the center of the vestibule. The floor was polished, black-

and-white Italian marble, and gilt-framed artwork of horses by sporting artist George Stubbs lined the walls. Sophia didn't miss Jane's flinch at the numerous colored stallions depicted in rampant splendor. Charles's stables had been full of horses.

Beyond the entrance was a winding staircase with an ornate balustrade leading to a second floor, gold-leafed balcony. Footsteps echoing off the marble floor drew Sophia's attention. Her chest tightened as Lord Delmont arrived in the vestibule to greet his guests.

"Welcome." Edward Black, Viscount Delmont, shook Robert's hand. He appeared to have gained two stone in weight since the masquerade party two weeks ago. His massive frame dominated the room. His brown eyes appeared small and beady in his beefy face.

Delmont turned his attention to her. "Lady Sophia. The last time I saw you, you were a scrap of a girl. It's been years."

Not as long as you think! She was thankful he remained completely ignorant of her presence the night of the masquerade.

His intense brown eyes raked her from head to toe with ill-disguised interest before he raised her hand to his lips. "I'm sorry for the loss of your father. Lord Haverton was a good friend."

She understood that several members of the Inventors' Society knew of her father's death, but not the specifics regarding the opium or the brothel in St. Giles where his body was found. The Marquess of Wendover was powerful enough to keep the details secret.

But Delmont would have known everything.

"Thank you, my lord." Bile rose in her throat, and she felt strangely light-headed.

Dear Lord! Don't faint! She'd never passed out in her life, and it took all her self-control not to rip her hand from Delmont's grasp as his lips made contact with her glove. Her skin crawled beneath the satin.

Robert appeared by her side, and propriety demanded the viscount release her hand.

"Lady Sophia and I are engaged to be married," Robert said.

Surprise flashed across Delmont's face before the smooth smile was back in place. "Congratulations, Kirkland," he said, stepping aside. "The men are in the library smoking cheroots. Come join us while your bags are delivered to your room. My wife will see to the ladies." He motioned for Robert to follow him just as his wife descended the grand staircase.

Vivian Black, Viscountess Delmont, came forward and smiled at Jane and Sophia. In contrast to her husband's height and girth, she was a thin, small-boned woman with dyed-red hair and a heavily painted face. She was dressed in flamboyant yellow silk with a jeweled-and-feathered turban.

"Welcome," she said, kissing the air around Sophia and Jane's cheeks with flourish.

Sophia forced a smile, and with iron determination kept her eyes from straying to the other woman's tall turban, adorned with yellow feathers and large tiger-eye stones.

The viscountess waved a hand. "I have planned an exciting week of entertainment. No ordinary musicales or boring poetry readings will take place, I assure you. I'm certain you will both enjoy yourselves. Lady Abagail Maxwell and Lady Beatrice Falk have already arrived."

Sophia knew both women, and their husbands had

been acquaintances of her father. They were also business partners and official stationers for the Regent, and they had each recently been bestowed with a baronetcy.

"Mrs. Stuart, my housekeeper, will show you to your rooms," the viscountess said.

A plump woman with a steel-gray bun came forward, a large wire ring of keys dangling from her fingers.

Sophia and Jane followed her up a winding staircase and down a long hall. They passed more than a dozen doors, and Sophia wondered just how many chambers existed in the mansion.

The housekeeper selected one of fifty keys in her key ring, opened a door, and ushered them inside. Two four-posters stood side by side, each with a sheer silk canopy of lavender. The walls were a darker shade of purple and the furnishings a rich mahogany. An adjoining sitting room door stood ajar.

"I hope it is to your satisfaction. Should you need anything, the bellpull is in the sitting room. Dinner will be served at seven," Mrs. Stuart said before departing.

Jane whirled around, her mouth agape. "It's a beautiful room."

Bitterness struck Sophia. The country residence was a display of Delmont's wealth and security. The guests would admire him; they had no notion of his criminal acts.

"It's almost too lavish," she said, a note of mockery in her voice.

Jane eyed her, a frown marring her brow. "What's wrong?"

"Forgive me," Sophia said. "It must be the travel." Pushing aside a fistful of lavender silk, she sat on one of the beds. "How long have you known the viscountess?"

"At least five years now. Since Charles joined the Inventors' Society." Jane opened a trunk that had been delivered and shook out a morning dress.

"The viscountess strikes me as a bit…how can I phrase it?"

"Odd," Jane finished.

Sophia arched an eyebrow.

"Vivian is a self-proclaimed medium," Jane said.

"A medium?"

"She claims to have communed with Cleopatra, Mark Antony, and Caesar in an attempt to clarify one of history's most famous love triangles."

Sophia stared at her. "That's ridiculous!"

Jane shrugged and pulled another dress from the trunk. "Vivian's eccentricity is overlooked because of her marriage to the viscount, the respectable head of the Society, and her impeccable bloodline, which can be traced back to Queen Elizabeth."

Sophia was struck by just how difficult a task Robert was undertaking. To arrest and successfully prosecute a peer of the realm—an influential leader of the Inventors' Society to boot—required solid proof. Viscount Delmont was no fool, but a cunning criminal who had evaded suspicion.

She stood and went to the door. "I need to stretch my legs."

Jane dropped the dress in her hands and turned to her. "Don't you want to change from your traveling gown? Dinner is—"

"I'll be back in time," Sophia promised.

Without further explanation, she left the room. Her immediate destination was the gardens where she could fill her lungs with fresh air and calm the chaos within her. Although her resolve had returned, she was still disturbed and shaken after seeing the viscount face-to-face.

Reliving his odious touch in her mind, she clenched her teeth and closed her eyes tight. Her intense physical reaction had been as disturbing as it had been out of character, and she berated herself for her weakness. If she was to successfully assist Robert in the investigation, then she would have to do much, much better.

She was halfway down the hall when a door swung open and a strong hand grasped her arm and pulled her into a dark room. Her back pressed against a solid chest, and a hand clamped over her mouth.

"Shh."

Instantly she knew it was Robert. His voice, his scent... even the feel of him was becoming intimately familiar.

She nodded, and he removed his hand.

He leaned down to whisper in her ear. "Are you all right?"

She turned and tilted her head up at him. "Why wouldn't I be?"

He eyed her speculatively. "You looked pale as death when Delmont greeted us."

"It had nothing to do with Delmont," she lied. "I don't travel well."

"Listen, Sophia. It's one thing to act as my betrothed at the Cameron's ball and another entirely to continue the charade under Delmont's roof. Will you be able to carry out your part or do you need to leave?"

"I'm made of sterner stuff, my lord."

"Nonetheless, avoid being alone with the viscount. I didn't like the way he looked at you."

What is that supposed to mean? She had the same

feelings, but to hear it spoken aloud by Robert sent a shiver of revulsion down her spine.

"The viscountess is here. Surely he wouldn't try anything with his own wife under his roof and risk—"

Robert's tone turned cold. "Do not underestimate him. You of all people know what he is capable of."

She swallowed hard.

"Where were you headed?"

"To the gardens."

"I'll escort you."

"No!"

When his lips parted to protest, she said, "Please, I'll be fine. We must follow propriety, remember? If you accompany me, then so must Jane."

He remained silent, glaring at her intensely.

"Shouldn't you return to the men before you are missed?" she pressed.

His eyebrows drew downward. "All right. But do not endanger yourself this week."

"I hardly think a walk in the gardens is endangering my—"

His eyes glinted like fine steel. "Don't think, just obey."

Chapter Ten

"Lord Kirkland! I didn't know you would be in attendance."

Robert was conscious of the attention from the guests as he walked across the drawing room.

"Sir Falk, it's good to see you again." He extended his hand to a short, portly man with a full head of unruly jet hair.

Falk pumped his hand. "I was glad to hear that you remain at the ordinance department after your uncle's and cousin's passing. The government needs men like you."

"Thank you. I understand your partner is present this week as well," Robert said.

At the mention of Sir Maxwell, a frown creased Sir Falk's brow.

"It's true." Maxwell, a tall, thin man with a pox-scarred face said as he approached. His bald scalp shone beneath the chandelier.

"How's business?" Robert asked. He had worked with

Maxwell and Falk in the past and knew they were issued a royal warrant as official stationers for the Crown. He had previously commissioned paper from them bearing the watermark of the ordinance department. From what he recalled, the partners were as opposite in personality as they were in appearance. The pair had always been amusing, but there was a definite tension between them tonight that Robert hadn't previously sensed.

Two women came up and Sir Falk made the introductions. "This is Beatrice, my wife. Abagail is Maxwell's wife."

The ladies acknowledged Robert with nods.

The drawing-room door opened and Sophia and Jane entered arm in arm. They looked lovely, but Robert's gaze lingered over Sophia's form in the amethyst gown. She had changed from her plain traveling dress for the evening meal, and the hugging silk emphasized her feminine curves and willowy height. Her hair was fashionably upswept and revealed the graceful curve of her nape. Crystal beads adorned the bodice, drawing his eyes to the swell of her breasts.

He intended to act the polite gentleman, then mentally dismiss her and focus on the cast of characters in attendance, but he found his attention riveted. Sophia possessed indefinable qualities that gave her a unique aura, very different from the women he had encountered in the past.

What was it about her?

She was beautiful. But he had met countless women even more beautiful than Sophia, whom he had effortlessly resisted.

She was highly intelligent. Others were smart.

She was strong-minded, opinionated, and determined.

Many men would deem these undesirable traits in a female.

She possessed courage and a charming vulnerability. Perhaps it was the odd combination of these two. He didn't know. All he was certain of was his attraction toward her.

And tonight, she looked, quite simply, like an expensive courtesan, innocent and alluring at once, a deadly combination for a man who had battled the demons inside him for as long as he could remember.

He motioned for her and Jane to approach. "I assume you know both Lady Sophia and Lady Stanwell. Lady Sophia and I are to be married," he said.

Congratulations were offered. He didn't miss the appreciative glances of the men.

A footman announced dinner was ready and the guests shuffled into the dining room.

Robert escorted Sophia and Jane to their assigned chairs before taking his own seat beside Sophia. Her skirts brushed his thigh and her perfume, a subtle scent of roses, wafted to him.

The remainder of the guests had arrived, fifteen in all, including the wives. The elegant dining room could easily sit fifty, but the house party was intended to be an intimate gathering of the Inventors' Society. He knew their numbers were greater, but Delmont had only invited a select group.

Why these men? Robert thought.

The viscount was last to sit at the head of the table, and his large girth barely fit between the armrests of his chair.

Sophia stiffened at the sight of their host. Candlelight gleamed in her chestnut curls. She looked uneasy, and he knew she was having misgivings. Despite her impetuous nature, she was struggling, and he felt himself wanting to ease her.

Damn. At a time he needed to concentrate on the guests seated before him, he was entranced by the lady beside him.

His fiancée.

He wanted to laugh at the thought. She was no more his than any of the countless women he had bedded before meeting Gwendolyn.

Robert leaned down to whisper in her ear. "Don't look at him."

She raised wide jade eyes to his.

"Look at me if it helps."

She shook her head slightly, and her lips parted.

He gave her no opportunity to speak, but squeezed her thigh beneath the table.

She sat up stiff as a statue.

"Remember, we are a loving couple," he reminded her.

He knew his tactic worked when her eyes flashed with green fire and color flooded her cheeks. He would much rather deal with an impetuous, bold Sophia than a fearful, vulnerable one.

He was not the only one to notice the change in her demeanor. Jane leaned forward and shot him a disapproving glare.

"Welcome guests," Delmont's voice boomed from the head of the table. "The viscountess and I have planned an exciting week of entertainment. There will be no musicales or dances. We are inventors, and we will celebrate our creative natures." He raised his wineglass. "But first we eat."

There was a collective nod from the guests as they raised their own glasses.

The dining room door opened and a line of liveried footmen in gold brocade carrying platters of beef, pork, fowl, salmon, and accompanying sauces marched into the room like a well-trained militia. The steaming platters were set upon a long sideboard laden with a dozen silver chafing dishes. Once the food was ready to be served, each footman stationed himself behind a couple.

Delmont's personal footman must have been accustomed to his master's demands, for within seconds his plate was heaped with meats and an assortment of buttered vegetables; his own basket of pastries sat beside the overladen plate. Expensive wine flowed freely, and the footmen ensured a guest's glass was never empty.

For a few minutes there was silence but for the *chink* of plates and cutlery. Robert took the opportunity to study the men.

Beside Delmont sat Lord and Lady Cameron, whose ball Robert and Sophia had waltzed at days ago. Maxwell and Falk and their wives were seated nearby.

As for the other guests, they were a mix of titled men, landed gentry, and wealthy merchants. The Society did not discriminate based on title, but all the inventors here were men of wealth, whether their money was inherited or earned in the London Stock Exchange or in business. Robert understood that inventing took capital, no matter the source of the money.

He wondered if the mastermind was present. Or was he an anonymous ringleader who issued orders from afar and did not participate openly with the group?

The viscount set down his fork. "It's my pleasure to welcome new members, Mr. George Brass and Mr. Henry Heinz. Mr. Brass is a successful silversmith and jeweler who is a talented engraver. Mr. Heinz has recently moved from Germany, and he owns several patents for fast burning gunpowder as well as his innovations to Joseph von Fraunhofer's spectroscope." Delmont glanced at Robert. "And I am happy to announce that Lord Kirkland has petitioned for membership. May you find this week's activities further pique your interest."

Robert smiled blandly, then proceeded to scrutinize each man. Brass looked to be in his late sixties, his face a battlefield of wrinkles and dark hair peppered with gray. His wife, on the other hand, appeared to be less than half his age. She was pleasant enough to look upon with brown hair and eyes, but her coloring was bland and her features plain. A man would not consider her beautiful, and she paled in comparison to both Sophia and Jane. Mrs. Brass must have sensed this for her lips thinned and her eyes narrowed whenever she looked in their direction.

Heinz, on the other hand, was in his thirties, with a head of thick brown hair and wire-rimmed spectacles that gave him the appearance of an Oxford professor.

"I'm especially pleased Mr. Brass has joined our group," Delmont said. "I've been after him for quite some time and I do believe he will find membership quite advantageous."

Mrs. Brass's painted lips smiled knowingly, and she nudged her elderly husband's arm. As the guests raised their glasses and offered congratulations, Delmont cast a glance not at Brass and Heinz, but at Sophia. His dark eyes boldly appraised her and rested on the swell of her breasts in the rounded bodice.

Robert's gut clenched, and myriad emotions churned within him. For one, Delmont desired Sophia. Robert didn't like it. The viscount was dangerous and cunning. Most likely a cold-blooded murderer. Second, the woman was a distraction to his mission, and for the hundredth time, he wondered what had addled Wendover's brain when he insisted they work together.

At last dinner drew to a close. Robert expected the men to stay and drink port and smoke cigars while the women waited for them in the drawing room. But custom did not take place here.

The viscountess stood, the feathers in her turban swaying. "We have planned an adventurous evening."

"It's a ship battle," Delmont said.

"Ooooh!" a group of ladies tittered.

The guests rose and followed the Delmonts through the open French doors leading to the back gardens. Vivian stopped beside a round, man-made pond, and the guests gathered around. Four model frigates floated in the water, two bearing the English flag, two others bearing flags of France and Spain.

Delmont joined his wife. "One of our members is working on improving the rigging on ships, and he has generously supplied the models. Mr. Heinz has supplied the gunpowder for our demonstration. The chosen war will be the 1805 Battle of Trafalgar."

The viscountess held out a fistful of sticks. "Four gentlemen will draw straws to determine armies."

One by one the chosen men approached to draw straws. Mr. Heinz and Sir Maxwell were pleased to have drawn the longest straws, which ensured them the model frigates bearing the English flag. Sir Falk and Mr. Brass frowned at drawing the shorter sticks, which gave them the French and Spanish frigates.

"Shall we commence?"

The spectators clapped.

Robert watched as the combatants used eight-foot-long poles to move their model ships around the circular pond, which was approximately twenty feet in diameter. Each model was equipped with three miniature cannons loaded with a trace of Mr. Heinz's special blend of gunpowder with an extra pinch of saltpeter.

At first, the men walked slowly around the perimeter of the pond, learning how best to maneuver their ships with the unwieldy poles. Mr. Heinz, the youngest in the group, was quickest to catch on.

"When a captain is ready to attack, a footman will assist by handing each man a separate, lit pole to light the fuse for their cannons," Delmont instructed.

Soon the spirit of competition took over, and the spectators cheered when the French frigate nearly collided with the Spanish. Wagers were immediately made.

This should be interesting, Robert mused. There was nothing like a "friendly competition" to discern who was the most cutthroat among the group.

"Trafalgar was England's most decisive sea battle off the coast of Spain. Admiral Lord Nelson was a genius!" Delmont shouted.

As if on cue, Sir Maxwell's frigate began attacking Sir Falk's at right angles.

"Nelson's method of attack was similar. It was a new tactic," Delmont said.

Sir Falk immediately tried to counterattack, but with his short legs and arms reaching as far as possible with his pole into the pond, he had trouble maneuvering his frigate. The pole slipped from his hand. His face glistened with perspiration.

Just then Maxwell lit his first fuse and seconds later, his miniature cannon blasted Falk's rigging. The frigate lurched, but stayed afloat.

"Damn you!" Falk shot a black look at Maxwell.

I was right, Robert thought. *They are hardly amicable.* The knowledge could be useful.

The crowd cheered at the first display of "drawn blood." He watched Sophia lean over the water, her green eyes flashing in excitement, her full lips parted. A curl had come loose from her coronet and caressed the tops of her breasts above the beaded bodice. The hem of her gown was perilously close to getting wet as she enthusiastically cheered for her favorite.

Robert noticed Delmont's large frame shift across the pond. The viscount's hot gaze was not focused on the sea battle, but on Sophia, and he licked his lips. She seemed blissfully unaware of his prurient interest as she continued to shout out.

Bloody hell. Robert would have to do something about her. But what? Emotion had no part in his duties. He must act dispassionately in order to ensure the success of this mission. He had learned firsthand that emotions resulted in weakness that could easily turn deadly.

A shot from another cannon drew Delmont's attention back to the battle. Robert watched as Mr. Brass blew a hole the size of a shilling in Mr. Heinz's frigate. The English ship slowly sank in the murky depths of the pond.

The battle went on for an additional half hour. The tiny cannons were not designed to sink the frigates quickly and before it was over each remaining miniature ship had numerous holes above the water level. It was Maxwell's last cannon blast that finally shot a big enough hole in Falk's frigate to cause it to sink.

"England wins!" the crowed chanted, as winning wagers were paid.

"Back to the house for sweets and wine," the viscountess said.

The group followed their hosts.

Robert pretended to follow last, but ducked behind one of the hedges. Hidden from view, he went still and listened.

"It was luck that you won." Falk's voice.

"Don't be an ass. No one likes a sore loser," Maxwell said smugly.

"You're bitter because Delmont favors me," Falk spat, then stalked off.

Robert waited until Maxwell huffed past before heading back to the house. Sophia was waiting for him beside the French doors. She studied him, her lips parted, petal soft and virginal pink. "The men are off drinking port in the library, and the women are in the drawing room."

"Then I bid you good night."

"Wait. What shall I do?" she asked eagerly.

He was again reminded of her inexperience in espionage. "Exactly what Wendover advised. Talk to the women."

He tried to walk by her, but she grasped his arm. His nostrils flared as he breathed in her intoxicating scent.

Her perfume reminded him of a garden of summer roses.

It made him think of where she dabbed it...her wrists, the slender column of her throat, in between her breasts. *Jesu*! It was like she was trying to test his will. Had she any idea the effect she had on him? Looking into emerald eyes, he saw unwavering spirit and innocence.

"What about you?" she asked.

"What about me?" His voice was harsh to his own ears.

She sighed impatiently. "What are *you* going to do while I'm talking to the ladies?"

"Don't concern yourself."

"You're not going to tell me anything, are you?"

"I told you before, I work alone."

Her glorious eyes flashed in defiance. "I told you before, I don't care."

"Sophia?"

Footsteps sounded on the marble floor, and Jane came around the corner. She halted, her lips parting in surprise at seeing Sophia alone with him. "Good evening, my lord. Did you enjoy the entertainment?" she asked.

His lips compressed. "It was as fascinating as it was unusual."

"Yes, it was," Jane said.

"I was just bidding Sophia good night." He gallantly bowed to them before departing.

• • •

By the time Sophia joined the women in the drawing room she was in a foul mood. Taking a seat beside Emma Brass, Sophia feigned interest in the women's talk of the latest French fashions and sipped her wine.

Stay out of his business, be damned! She refused to play a passive role when it was her father's murder Robert was investigating.

She understood Robert's hesitation after her show of fear at seeing Viscount Delmont for the first time since the masquerade ball. Her initial anxiety about being in close proximity to him was not entirely gone, but she now knew how to mask her emotions.

She would not be put in her place like a fresh-faced debutante out of the schoolroom. She was twenty-four years old, and she had survived sharing a meal with her father's murderer. She would do whatever it took to see those responsible pay. She just needed to convince Robert of her usefulness and unwavering resolve.

If only he weren't so attractive. She wondered if she would ever get used to looking at him. But that was part of his persona, wasn't it? The man could transform himself from cunning spy into a charming gentleman with efficient ruthlessness. His looks were just another weapon in his arsenal.

She straightened her spine and clenched the wineglass. She had never been one to take no for an answer when she truly desired something. Hadn't she slipped into Delmont's masquerade unnoticed? Hadn't she found her way into the viscount's guarded wing and private study that night? If Robert thought to ignore her and set her aside, then he was in for a rude awakening.

After the ship battle she had tried to tell him she intended to play a bigger role in the investigation. But Jane had interrupted.

She would wait until tonight, after the men and women retired for the evening, before slipping out of her room to have a private word with him.

Chapter Eleven

Robert knew precisely where to begin his search that night. Tossing aside his boots, he lay in his bed fully clothed—arms folded behind his head, legs crossed at the ankles.

He waited until the mantle clock displayed the hour he'd awaited—two in the morning. The guests would be fast asleep in their rooms to be well rested for a hunt that Delmont had announced would take place in the morning.

He rose and slipped out of the room. The servants had long ago snuffed the candles in the wall sconces. Only one candle burned low at the end of the hall by the balcony leading to the winding staircase. He preferred the night, and his eyes and ears were well attuned to flickering shadows on the flocked wallpaper and the slight creak of a floorboard.

He descended the grand stairs and stepped into the vestibule. The Italian marble was cool beneath his stockinged feet. Turning the corner, he walked down the long hall and stopped before Delmont's study.

The door was closed, and no light shone beneath it. He turned the handle and slipped inside.

More darkness.

The smell of linseed oil and leather furniture permeated the space. Reaching into his pocket, he pulled out a candle and lit a match. The small glow revealed closed velvet curtains across a window behind a desk. Two leather armchairs were situated before a stone fireplace; directly across from the chairs a sofa rested against the east wall. A large world globe sat upon an end table in the corner beside the sofa.

Lighting a lamp with his candle, he circled the study. Wendover's map had indicated the safe was most likely located behind a Gainsborough portrait. But a quick glance behind the gilt frame confirmed Robert's suspicions.

Nothing. Delmont was too savvy for such a predictable location.

Rolling back an Oriental carpet, he found the safe beneath the sofa.

A floor safe?

Considering the viscount's size and girth it was an unlikely location. Robert's lips twitched as an image of Delmont struggling on his hands and knees to open the lock came to him.

Placing the lamp on a floorboard beside the safe, he crouched to examine the Barron lever-tumbler lock, named after its inventor Robert Barron. The lock was cleverly recessed so that it would not create a noticeable lump in the carpet should the sofa be moved.

Robert withdrew his lock picks from his pocket and laid them on the floorboards. He chose a long thin rod and slipped it into the lock. Using a "tickling" technique, he carefully maneuvered each of the five levers in the lock, raising them one by one to the correct height. Only when all five levers were raised and lined up in the correct height would the lock open.

It was a painfully slow process, but the best method to avoid destroying the lock. He could remove the contents and then close the safe with no one able to tell it had been tampered with.

But he had to be careful. The lock was spring-loaded. One wrong move—a fraction too high—and he could trigger the spring, causing a lever to snap down and prohibit further manipulation.

By the time he had raised four of the levers to the proper height, sweat beaded his brow. Crouching over his work, his back throbbed and the muscles between his shoulder blades ached. He had worked in worse conditions in the past, of course, and this wasn't his first difficult lock.

He took a deep breath, closed his eyes and concentrated on the pick in his hand.

Focus. This wasn't any different from the hundreds of safes he'd opened before.

At last the lever rose and he was rewarded with a slight *click* as the lock opened.

Just then voices sounded outside the door.

He snuffed out the lamp and froze. Damn. He had been so engrossed in the safe he hadn't heard footsteps. Crouching behind the sofa, the room was dim save for a sliver of moonlight from the cracked curtains.

He hoped it was servants passing, uninterested in the study. He would not relish being forced to incapacitate anyone in order to preserve his anonymity. He strained to hear, his heart pounding.

"*Lady Sophia, what are you doing up wandering the halls?*"

Robert recognized Delmont's voice. The viscount's question reverberated through Robert's mind as well. What *was* she doing up?

"*Pardon, my lord,*" Sophia said. "*I couldn't sleep and thought to get some warm milk from the kitchen.*"

"*You should have called for a servant.*"

"*I didn't want to inconvenience anyone my first night here.*"

"*Nonsense.*"

"*Why are you up, my lord?*"

"*Please call me Edward. I often spend time in my study late at night.*"

"*I admit I'm glad you found me, Edward. I tend to be frightened of the dark. If it's not too much trouble, perhaps you can escort me back to my room.*"

"*I'd be honored.*"

Christ! Robert suspected what Sophia was up to. She had somehow followed him and knew he was in the study accessing the safe. She was flirting with the viscount, encouraging his attentions in an effort to aid him.

He should be thankful, yet he felt anything but gratitude. The emotions surging through his veins were as uncomfortable as they were unfamiliar. He struggled with the ridiculous urge to burst through the study door and strangle Delmont with his bare hands.

Snatching up the contents of the safe—a single folded sheet of paper—he held it up to the moonlight, but there wasn't enough light to read the small script. He dared not linger. Refolding the paper, he tucked it into his pocket.

Just before he closed the door, a glint of gold at the bottom of the safe caught his eye. Reaching down, he picked up a small gold gear. It was identical to the ones Wendover had found on the bodies of the murdered inventors. He returned it to the safe and secured the lock.

Opening the study door, he blended into the shadows.

...

"I'm grateful you found me tonight, my lord," Sophia said.

Delmont's gaze raked her nightgown and wrapper. He carried a lamp, and the glow illuminated the lust in his eyes. Although the cotton covered every inch of her person and was demure, clearly his thoughts were not.

"It's Edward, remember?" he said hoarsely.

"Yes, Edward," she breathed.

Looking up into Delmont's florid face, she feigned an ease she didn't feel. She had left her room in the middle of the night intending to confront Robert. But when she had knocked on his bedchamber door and he did not answer, she knew he was prowling the house, sneaking into rooms—doing what he did best.

She had wondered where he would start. The study was her first guess. She'd crept downstairs and was making her way along the hall where a faint light beneath the study's closed door had confirmed her suspicions. Before she could press her ear to the door, the scrape of booted feet sounded on the marble tile. Seconds later, the viscount's large frame had turned the corner.

Flee, her mind had screamed. But through the sickening

panic that tied her guts in knots, an inner voice of reason had prevailed.

Robert needed her.

Little by little, warmth crept back into her along with a plan. The study couldn't be the only room that held Delmont's secrets. Robert would require opportunity, and if that meant distracting the viscount, then she could ensure that Robert had all the time he needed. Maybe then he would treat her as an equal partner in the investigation.

Under the guise of returning to her room, she steered the viscount away from the study.

"Pray tell me, why couldn't you sleep tonight?" Delmont asked.

She hesitated and licked her bottom lip. Instantly his eyes were drawn to her mouth.

"I was thinking of my father," she whispered.

They reached the bottom of the grand staircase. He held the lamp high, and the light flickered off his dark eyes. "My dear Sophia. It must be difficult for a young, unmarried lady to live alone."

"I am to be married to Lord Kirkland soon."

Something disturbing replaced his smoldering look. "Nevertheless, I insist you come to me for anything."

"Is that proper?"

"Lord Kirkland is new to the title. I am older and established and can open many doors in society for you." He touched her cheek, then lowered his hand to her shoulder. "It will be our secret. No one needs to know."

Her skin crawled beneath the cotton. "The viscountess is a fortunate woman."

The reminder of his wife did nothing to cool his look of

lust. "I shall escort you to your door."

"No!" She touched his sleeve to soften her words. "No thank you, Edward. My cousin, Lady Stanwell, is sharing my chambers. I wouldn't want anyone to learn of our new friendship. I do wish to see you again."

His eyes smoldered. "Soon," he urged.

"Yes, soon," she promised, then fled up the stairs.

...

Once alone in his bedchamber, Robert didn't have to wait long. A soft knock sounded, and he opened the door.

Sophia stood in her nightgown and wrapper, and although the embroidered, white cotton covered her from her neck to her wrists down to her dainty slippers, he froze as if she had appeared stark naked at his door.

He might be celibate by choice, but he wasn't a monk, and his eyes were drawn to the swell of her breasts, the voluptuous curve of her hips. With the flickering candlelight behind her, he could make out the shape of a hip, a long, slender leg. Her hair was loose, a bounty of chestnut tresses any red-blooded male would long to touch as he kissed her full lips.

His groin tightened, and he felt the inevitable stirrings of lust. He scowled at the thought that Delmont had seen her dressed like this, had been alone with her in the dim halls.

He motioned her inside with a jerk of his hand and shut the door.

She whirled to face him. "What did you find?"

"What were you thinking?"

"I thought to find you."

"Why?"

"I told you. I won't be put aside. My father was murdered. I have a right to be involved, and it's not in my nature to sit back and do nothing. I refuse to obey your ridiculous orders."

His eyes narrowed. "I was right. Your rashness is dangerous."

Every curve of her body spoke defiance. "If it wasn't for my rashness, you would have been caught."

"I won't deny you prevented the viscount from walking into his study, but I can handle myself."

"How? By killing him?"

"That would have been unwise. It would definitely have put the mastermind on notice. I would have used other means to disable him. He never would have seen me."

She bit her bottom lip. "I see."

His voice hardened. "Stay away from Delmont."

"Please, at least tell me what you found."

He hesitated, then decided it was better to give her the information. He had no intention of fully involving her in his investigation, but if she knew which men were involved, then she could best draw out their wives as well as take appropriate measures to protect herself. He withdrew the folded sheet from his waistcoat pocket and handed it to her.

"What is it?"

"A list of names."

She unfolded the paper and scanned it. "Maxwell and Falk and several others are listed." She looked up at him. "You think these are members of a select, secret group amongst the Inventors' Society?"

"Yes. There was also one gold gear in the safe, similar to

the ones found on the dead men."

"Perhaps it belongs to the mastermind."

He shook his head. "I don't think so. I believe one more member is to be inducted. I suspect it will happen this week."

"It could be meant for one of the new members, Mr. Brass or Mr. Heinz," she pointed out.

"Or maybe one of the older members, like Lord Cameron," he said.

The color drained from her face. "Not Lord Cameron! He was my father's good friend."

Robert let out a slow breath. "Sophia, I never did tell you, but I am sorry about Haverton's death. He was a good man."

Her voice wavered. "You knew my father?"

"We met briefly on several occasions."

The change in topic had clearly caught her off guard. Her green eyes widened, deep pools of appeal a man could drown in.

Control yourself, man! Think of Gwendolyn.

Sophia was no different from any of the women who had tested his will. He had resisted them all, just as he would her.

She touched his sleeve, and he started to sweat, almost as much as when he had crouched over the Barron lock.

"The list is a good start," he said, steering the conversation away from her father, the one topic that made her lower lip tremble and pain flicker in her eyes. She appeared vulnerable and withdrawn, a woman in need of comfort.

But he was not the man to give her what she needed, dammit.

"If we know who the members are we can watch them and discern what they are up to. The answer may be in the viscount's other safes," he said.

She lifted her eyes, once again focused on the task rather than any painful memories. "How else can I help?"

"The women, remember?"

"Right. Lady Maxwell and Lady Falk are talkative. I'll start with them." She tilted her head, studying him. "But I want to do more. What about Delmont's bedchamber? My father always kept his letters patents and other important documents in his room. I can distract the viscount while you—"

"No. I told you to stay away from Delmont," he growled.

If she was taken aback by his harsh tone, she did not show it. Handing him back the list of names, she asked, "Won't Delmont notice this missing from his safe?"

"I'm returning it tonight."

"You're going back?"

"Yes. Don't follow me."

"Isn't that dangerous? What if Delmont returns?"

At the sight of her obvious distress, something odd lurched in his chest. It had been a long, long time since anyone had cared. He couldn't help himself; he raised her chin with his thumb. "I've done this countless times before."

"I wouldn't want anything to happen to you. How would I reach Wendover?"

"There will be no need. I'm now familiar with the feel of the lock. It will take me half the time."

She nervously licked her lips. "Still, I don't—"

His thumb rubbed across her glistening bottom lip. He had the insane urge to suck the tempting flesh into his mouth, to slip his tongue inside hers...to ravenously kiss her.

She gasped, looking just as startled as he felt, but she

didn't move, didn't slap his hand away…didn't step back.

Ludicrous. She would drive him completely mad.

He felt himself slipping where he had gone only once before, and he immediately recoiled at the thought. Emotional attachment was not an option. Yet he felt a crack in his hardened armor. Closing the door wasn't sufficient; he had to slam it shut, no matter how brutal the method, or in this case, how cruel the words.

Dropping his hand, he took a step back. "Your concern is touching, but you should be careful. I just may think you're no different from all my other female admirers and are starting to like me."

Something flashed in her eyes—disappointment? confusion?—but to his relief, the fleeting emotion was gone, and her face reddened with anger.

"Again, you flatter yourself, my lord."

"Flattery has nothing to do with it. Do not soften toward me. Despite what Wendover said, I'm not a man you can trust with your virtue."

Her mouth gaped.

He opened the door. "Go now before Jane wakes to find you missing."

To his relief, she didn't argue, but whirled and left his room.

Chapter Twelve

Deep in the recesses of Robert's subconscious, he knew he was having another nightmare, but he lacked the wherewithal to force himself awake. It started the same, it always did, and no matter how hard he tried to alter the ending of the nightmare, he had never succeeded.

The urgency to arrive on time hummed in his veins, in his blood, in his essence. The clock ticking in his mind—each minute…each second, they all mattered.

It was supposed to be his last mission. He had told Wendover of his resignation. A married man was not one who could take the daily risks required in his work for the Home Office.

His orders were clear. Assassinate the Comte DeForte, a double agent and a man in league with Napoleon, and steal the covert military documents in his safe. He needn't bother with nondestructive manipulation and could blow the safe wide open. If he could simultaneously accomplish both tasks—obtain the papers and kill the Comte—then all the better.

He had planted the explosives. The gunpowder was in place. He had carefully positioned additional powder on the hinges of the safe to blow the door open without destroying its contents. A length of fuse snaked out the window to the gardens below where he lay in wait. He shifted beneath the bushes, the cold of the December earth seeping into his bones, his spyglass trained on the front door of the lavish country house. It was late afternoon, the rotation of the guards had taken place, and the Comte was expected to return home soon.

Robert heard the carriage wheels before the conveyance came into view up the stone drive.

Perfect.

He waited until the carriage door opened and Comte DeForte stepped out before striking flint to steel and setting a spark to the fuse.

The Comte turned and offered his hand to another occupant. A golden-haired woman appeared in the carriage doorway.

Gwendolyn.

Her porcelain features, slender frame, and the blond coronet of braids struck him like a blow to the solar plexus. Placing her hand on the Comte's sleeve, the couple went up the steps into the house.

Robert scrambled from under the bushes, but the fuse had already traveled like wildfire up to the second-floor window and out of reach. He sprinted across the lawn, shouting as he ran.

Seconds passed. An eternity.

The explosion reverberated in his head. Shattered glass rained down and flames burst through the windows. A barrage of roof slates and stone flew through the air with the force of cannon shot. Twenty yards from the structure, he fell to his knees, battered by debris, his shirt singed by shooting embers.

He struggled to his feet and ran toward the inferno, his arms and legs pumping, his chest straining with each step. He passed through the gaping hole where the door hung askew and into the vestibule. Heat blasted his face; smoke seared his lungs and burned his eyes. He took a step forward and tripped over a body. There lying at his feet was his wife.

Sweet Jesus!

Her face, her beautiful face.

Why? Why had she come here?

He was to blame. He had planted the explosives and was solely responsible.

Murderer! What kind of penance could make up for his sins?

He awoke drenched in sweat, his heart racing. Nauseous, he bent over the side of the bed, gasping in deep gulps of air.

Yes, no matter how hard he tried to alter the ending—at least in his nightmares—he had never succeeded.

. . .

The man was insufferable.

Sophia was still fuming over Robert's comment the following morning. The women were sitting in the Delmonts' lovely courtyard overlooking the front gardens. Large pots of flowering blooms splashed brilliant color against the white stone courtyard, and a striped awning offered shade from the sun. The weather was beautiful, the sky a brilliant blue, and the conversation amicable, but all she could think about was her heated discussion with Robert in his bedchamber last night.

He had accused her of starting to fall for his charm—similar to the countless other London ladies who had no doubt thrown themselves at his feet. She'd wanted to throttle him; she refused to think of her own physical reaction to his nearness.

Despite his assurances that he could have handled matters in the study, she knew she'd helped him by diverting Delmont. But rather than expressing gratitude, he had been reproachful.

Stay away from Delmont, he had warned.

Hadn't she proved she could handle herself and be an indispensible ally?

The rattling of a tea cart over the slate terrace drew her from her musings. A maid stopped the cart and began setting teacups and saucers before the women.

"Jane tells me you met Lord Kirkland while learning how to waltz," Abagail Maxwell said beside Sophia.

"Tsk. Such a scandalous dance," Beatrice Falk said.

"Oh, I think it's wonderful," Emma Brass said. "The waltz is so much more exciting than any country reel." She hesitated and tucked a loose curl behind her ear.

Lady Maxwell ignored the others and directed her attention to Sophia. "Your fiancé, Lord Kirkland, is quite charming."

Sophia reminded herself she was acting and sipped her tea before responding. "Yes, he is wonderful and I consider myself most fortunate for gaining his attention."

There was a flash of an indiscernible emotion in Emma Brass's eyes. Jealousy perhaps? Her husband had to be at least forty years older.

Sophia turned to her. "You were recently married?"

"Close to six months now," Emma said.

"I understand Mr. Brass is a silversmith and jeweler," Sophia said.

Emma's face lit up. "Oh, George is much more than just a shopkeeper. He is quite skilled at engraving. He can duplicate any print. You should see his replica of William Hogarth's *The Marriage Contract*. His own original artwork is exceptional as well. I keep telling him to meet with a reputable dealer who works with exhibitions at the Royal Academy of Arts."

Was she proud of her elder husband or merely ambitious?

Lady Falk spoke up. "The Royal Academy! That's truly beyond your husband's abilities. It exhibits only the best London artists. What would you know of art, Mrs. Brass?"

Emma colored fiercely. "I know what's pretty when I see it," she said defensively.

Lady Falk halted in the middle of adding sugar to her tea. "Humph."

"Never mind her, Mrs. Brass," Lady Maxwell said before whirling on Lady Falk. "Do keep your opinions to yourself, Beatrice. You're not always right."

"And I suppose you are?" Lady Falk retorted.

"What are you implying?" Lady Maxwell said.

Well, well, Sophia thought. The wives feud just like their spouses. She recalled the short, fat Sir Falk and the tall, thin Sir Maxwell battling it out with their ships in the pond. Not for the first time, she wondered how they could be successful business partners.

"There, there. Let's not ruin a lovely morning," Jane said, smoothing the women's ruffled feathers.

There was a moment of silence as they sipped their tea and nibbled on scones.

As Sophia raised her teacup, she saw the men at the edge of the woods returning from their hunt, mounted on prime horseflesh from the viscount's stables. Robert's attire was somber—gray jacket, white shirt, and matching trousers. She knew he made an effort not to draw attention to himself, but no amount of plain clothing could disguise his regal bearing and lean build. Sunlight set off the sparks of gold in his tawny hair and separated him from the pack.

As they rode past, he looked up at the terrace and spotted her. His lips curled in a smile and he raised a hand in greeting. His appeal was devastating, and her heart hammered foolishly. Aware of the audience, she waved back, then wrenched herself away from her ridiculous preoccupation with his face.

Emma Brass nodded in acknowledgement at Mr. Brass, but her countenance brightened as her eyes slid over Robert's person.

The French doors opened and Vivian Black, Lady Delmont, stepped onto the terrace. Dressed in a flowing gown of topaz, she wore a matching turban with a peacock feather that swayed in the slight breeze. "While the men drink their port and smoke their cigars after the evening meal, I have planned a séance for the ladies."

A hushed silence descended as the women took in the viscountess's statement.

Beatrice Falk was the first to speak. "A séance? Whatever

do you mean?"

"A group sitting where we attempt to contact the spirits," Vivian said.

"I've attended parties where a mesmerist was present, even a hypnotist, but I daresay I've never even *heard* of a séance," Abagail Maxwell protested.

Vivian surveyed the women. "We are wives of inventors. We must embrace new ideas. Our husbands frequently work with novel projects in their workshops. Why should we be any different?"

Beatrice's expression was tight with strain, her plump fingers tense in her lap. "Still—"

"Séances have been successfully conducted," Vivian said. "I have studied the writings of Swedish scientist Emanuel Swedenborg, German physician Franz Mesmer, and read Sir George Lyttelton's *Communication With the Other Side*. All have attempted to contact the spirit world. I have experience, and I will be your guide." At the continued silence, Vivian prodded, "Aren't any of you curious? Haven't any of you wanted to speak with a loved one who's passed away?"

Although apprehension and even fear crossed the women's faces, the viscountess's speech was persuasive. Lady Cameron sat forward in her seat; Mrs. Brass's eyes shone with eagerness.

The idea intrigued Sophia. A séance offered a unique setting to observe the others. Fear of the unknown offered the opportunity to bring out unexpected personality traits that could be much more revealing. Even Jane looked interested.

"Any suggestions as to whom I should attempt to contact this evening?" Vivian asked.

Outbursts immediately followed.

"My great-aunt Tilly!"

"My mother!"

"Aidan Webster!" Mrs. Brass shouted out. At several inquisitive looks, she blushed and said, "He was a family friend who perished at Waterloo."

Vivian held up a bejeweled hand. "I suggest each of you write down a name and place it in this hat." A footman came forward and held out a beaver hat. "I'll draw a name right before the séance begins. That way no one can be accused of having influenced my decision."

...

It was hours later before Sophia was finally able to speak with Jane alone. They had returned to their room to change for dinner and Sophia was contemplating the appropriate attire for a spiritual communication.

"What do you think of Mrs. Brass?" she asked, opening the wardrobe doors.

Jane picked up a silver-handled brush and began working it through her flaxen hair. "Emma Brass is hot-blooded and ambitious."

Sophia rolled her eyes. "I doubt the man she had mentioned for the séance was solely a family friend and soldier."

Jane giggled. "More like her former lover."

"I can't decide whether to like her or keep my guard around her," Sophia said.

"I wonder how Mr. Brass keeps up with her," Jane said.

Sophia chuckled. "I admit I thought the same thing. She isn't the only entertaining lady present. Lady Maxwell and Lady Falk just may stab each other with Delmont's fine silver over the dinner table."

"Their husbands are no better." Jane eyed Sophia. "Are you certain you wish to enter the state of matrimony yourself?"

Sophia answered without hesitation. "Quite. What about you?"

"Me?" Jane halted, the brush in her hands. "You can't be serious?"

"Why not? You're beautiful and young and have so much to offer."

"Even though you have forgotten the past, Sophia, I haven't. And society looks at me like I am a pestilence of despair."

Sophia waved her hand. "Society can go to the devil! There are men out there who don't give a fig about gossip."

A flicker of emotion flashed in Jane's brown eyes, but it was gone so quickly Sophia thought she must have imagined it.

What was Jane thinking? Or more like it, who was Jane thinking of?

"Regardless," Sophia said, "I'm happy to see you laugh again. Are you as excited for the séance as I am?"

"I admit I feel some of the initial apprehension voiced by Lady Maxwell. You don't honestly believe Lady Delmont can contact the dead, do you?" Jane asked.

"No, I don't. But that doesn't mean *she* doesn't believe it."

"Our hostess is quite unusual."

"More like cracked," Sophia said.

Jane laughed again, then fell quiet. "Some of the other women believe her. I wonder if—"

"No. If it were true, there would be a line of people at her door willing to pay any amount of money for her services,"

Sophia pointed out.

Jane sighed. "You're right, of course."

A low knock on the door announced the arrival of one of the Delmonts' maids. They finished dressing, and Sophia followed Jane downstairs. But when they entered the dining room, she realized she had forgotten to ask whose name Jane had put in the hat.

· · ·

Robert cornered Sophia after dinner and led her behind a potted palm in the parlor. "I heard about the séance," he said.

"I've never been part of one. The viscountess's pastime is quite novel."

"People have always been trying to contact the dead. I suspect the practice has yet to reach its peak." His expression turned sober. "Whom did you request to resurrect? Your father?"

She shook her head. "No. King Henry VIII."

He arched an eyebrow. "Not one of his wives?"

"I couldn't choose."

He chuckled. "See what you can find out about the others. A spiritualist meeting may reveal hidden secrets."

"I thought the same thing." The scent of his shaving soap teased her nostrils when she leaned close to whisper, "What are you up to tonight?"

He winked. "The manor has countless rooms to investigate."

· · ·

Robert slipped into Sir Falk's bedchamber while the men

were drinking their after dinner port, smoking cigars, and conducting experiments regarding magnetism and the effects on compasses.

As expected, there were no safes in the guest chambers. He searched the Falk's baggage, careful not to disturb the order of their contents or the way each article of clothing was folded. He had already rummaged through the Maxwell's belongings and found nothing of significance—no gold gears, incriminating lists, or sketches of military-worthy devices.

Maxwell and Falk were on the list of conspirators. So what was their plan?

He closed the baggage and was about to quit the room when he spotted a ream of paper under the wardrobe. Flipping through the stack, he noted that the sheets were all blank. Nothing unusual here, since Maxwell and Falk were stationers and made their living selling paper. Nonetheless, Robert's training had taught him to never overlook even a simple find. He held a sheet to the light. It was fine quality, white wove and bore the watermark F&M, distinguishing it as from their stock.

Perhaps the ream was for Delmont as a gift? It was clearly not commissioned. If had been, it would have a watermark bearing his crest.

He returned the paper beneath the wardrobe, then went to the window, opened the casement and stepped onto the ledge. He knew the layout of the house—the viscount's bedchamber was around the corner.

The ledge was ornate stone, only six inches wide. He carefully stepped past empty rooms, until he came to the right window. He dared a quick glimpse inside.

He was in luck. The chambermaid was inside and she

had opened the window while she tidied the room. He could hear her humming as she worked, oblivious to his presence. He waited until she entered the adjoining sitting room before swiftly climbing into the room and hiding behind a settee in the corner.

Her tasks finally completed, she closed the window and departed.

Seconds later, he emerged. He found the safe in a closet behind dozens of the viscount's hanging jackets. He expected to find money, jewels…a hint as to the mastermind's identity and the secret group's agenda.

He found a single, blank sheet of paper instead.

Similar to the ream in Falk's chamber, it was white, wove paper, not the cruder, less expensive laid stuff, but it lacked a watermark. He flipped the sheet over, looking for any marks, however small, he may have initially missed. He saw nothing.

Why hide a single sheet of foolscap?

Unless it did indeed have something written on it… something indiscernible to the human eye.

Robert recalled a bottle of invisible ink stashed in the desk drawer of his study. He used it to deliver messages to the Home Office. He often wrote with black ink over the invisible ink so that if the missive fell into the wrong hands it would not be suspected. The only way to see the ink was to heat the paper by holding a flame close to its surface.

He spotted a tinderbox on an end table by the bed and lit a candle. Heating the paper, he waited. Five seconds, then ten.

Nothing. Not a mark.

He frowned. What the devil?

If Delmont had yet to compose a message, then why lock up a blank sheet?

Chapter Thirteen

The séance was to take place in a room specifically designated for the viscountess's spiritual communications, on the first floor of an addition in the rear of the house. Circular in shape, the only way in or out was through the single door leading to the main part of the house. No French doors opened into the back gardens, and a single window was heavily draped, blocking out any moonlight.

The women walked inside. Several gasped; others froze in surprise. Sophia's eyes widened as she surveyed the scene. Dozens of candles glowed in the space. A large round table dominated the room. At first glance she thought the walls were painted black, then realized they were a deep burgundy—the color of blood.

Vivian was waiting by the table. Dressed in a flowing robe exactly the same shade of burgundy as the walls, her gold turban presented a striking contrast. Her dyed-red hair was unbound and fell down her back.

"Please take your seats," she instructed, before finding it necessary to prod the gaping women. "Hurry now! I've already prepared the room and I dare not keep the spirits waiting."

Sophia sat between Jane and Emma Brass.

The viscountess placed a glass bowl of water with a floating candle in the center of the table. "Water and fire are two of the essential elements. This shall be my focal point." Reaching for a tinderbox, she lit the candle in the bowl.

"It's time to pick our deceased." She held up the beaver hat from the morning. "Lady Cameron can do the honors."

Lady Cameron's face was tense, and her hand trembled as she reached in and pulled out a scrap of paper.

The viscountess plucked it from her and cleared her throat. "Charles Peckwick, the fifth Earl of Stanwell."

There was a collective gasp as all heads turned toward Jane. She stiffened and all color drained from her face.

Sophia touched Jane's sleeve. "Did you put Charles's name into the hat?"

Jane whimpered. "I did not! Who would do such a thing?"

The women eyed Jane with disbelief and pity. Sophia felt a simmering anger. She didn't know whether it was because the others doubted Jane's word or because of their ill-disguised pity. Did they truly believe Jane was the reason behind her husband's suicide?

"You must pick another name," Sophia said sharply.

"But someone here wishes to speak with him," Vivian said.

"It doesn't matter. His widow does not wish it," Sophia retorted. "Whoever put the earl's name in the hat was acting selfishly."

"I suppose if Jane is adamant about it, we shall choose another," Vivian said.

Jane stood. "Wait! Let us move forward. I do have something to say to my husband."

Sophia stared at Jane. "You don't have to do this. Nothing can come of it."

Jane squeezed Sophia's hand. "It's all right."

The viscountess nodded. "How very brave of you, Jane."

She then went around and snuffed all the other candles in the room. Smoke swirled in the air until the floating candle in the center of the round table was the only remaining light. The viscountess took her seat, and her gold turban glowed in the candlelight, highlighting her face, while her burgundy robe blended with the dark walls.

"Everyone hold hands and remain silent," Vivian directed.

Jane's grasp on Sophia's fingers was cold and tight, while Emma's was slightly damp.

Please don't let Jane think this could be real! Sophia thought.

She was afraid for her cousin. Jane's emotional state had been fragile since the suicide. She was just beginning to come out of her shell and enjoy life. What would this farce do to her?

For several seconds there was silence. The air seemed to vibrate with anticipation.

"I sense Charles's presence!" the viscountess said. She lifted her chin, her dark eyes bright in the flickering candlelight. "Charles! Charles, are you here?"

Silence.

"Charles!"

Sophia felt it then. A slight tremor in the table — a sort

of frisson that made the hair on her nape rise and gooseflesh appear on her arms. The tremor increased, shaking the glass bowl and making the floating candle flicker.

"Sweet Lord!" Lady Cameron cried out. "It's working."

Across the table, Lady Falk and Lady Maxwell's mouths fell open as they gaped at each other in alarm.

Sophia glanced at Jane. Her complexion was pale as parchment, her brown eyes wide in her delicate face.

Someone must be moving the table. Sophia looked to each woman, trying to discern who was responsible and how they were pulling off such a feat when Vivian's shout startled her.

"Yes! Yes! Charles is among us. Do not separate your hands, or you'll break contact with the spirit."

Air swirled around Sophia's silk shoes and ruffled the pleated hem of her gown. Had Jane or Emma Brass brushed against her? The women sat motionless, enthralled.

The viscountess raised her gaze to the center of the room, directly above the floating candle. All eyes followed her movement.

"I see his face. Red-gold curls, blue eyes…he always was a handsome one," Vivian said.

A strangled cry escaped from Jane.

"Are you at peace, Charles?" Vivian said.

The trembling of the table increased.

"He is caught in between death and the afterlife. He is trapped," Vivian said.

Emma Brass leaned toward Lady Falk. "Suicide is not sanctioned by the church."

In the quiet room, Sophia clearly heard her words. No doubt Jane had as well. Sophia wanted to slap the woman senseless.

"Charles's spirit is growing stronger, and his full form is taking shape. He is dressed elegantly in a moss waistcoat, ruffled shirt, striped stockings, and breeches. He is twirling his pocket watch, and there is a fob dangling with a bit of gold," Vivian said.

It was Sophia's turn to gasp. Was the viscountess describing a gold gear? Was it possible Charles had possessed one?

Had Charles been a member of the secret group?

"It is time. Who has questions for Charles?" Vivian asked.

All heads turned to Jane.

"Jane wasn't the one to put Charles's name in the hat," Sophia insisted.

"Anyone can ask questions," Vivian said.

Jane's mouth opened, then closed. Pushing back her chair, she rose, still clutching the hands of the women on either side of her. Her gaze never wavered from above the glass bowl where Charles's spirit supposedly hovered. Her lips parted to speak.

Just then the flame on the floating candle snuffed out and the room was plunged into complete blackness.

The women screamed and broke hands. The table ceased trembling.

Seconds passed, and Sophia heard flint strike iron. She blinked at the glow of light as the viscountess lit a wall sconce.

"The connection is broken. Charles is gone," Vivian proclaimed.

Sophia glanced to her right.

Jane was, too.

Chapter Fourteen

Sophia flew down the hall and headed straight for Robert's room. At her panicked rapping, the door swung open. Powerful relief filled her that he was present. Without a doubt, she knew he would be able to help.

He was obviously changing from an outing, and his starched shirt was only partly buttoned, revealing the corded muscles of his throat and a tanned V of flesh. A jacket of blue superfine hung on a knob from the chest of drawers.

A glance at her face made his blue eyes narrow. "What's wrong?"

"Please, you must help. The séance was a disaster. Jane locked our chamber door and won't answer. I need to get inside." She knew she was blabbering, but she was truly frightened for her cousin.

Robert clasped her shoulders and led her into the room. He kicked the door shut with a booted foot and sat her in an armchair by the fireplace. Kneeling beside her, he looked into her eyes. "Take a deep breath, and start from the beginning."

She quickly summarized the evening's events.

"If Jane believes Charles's spirit was summoned," Robert said, "then she is in shock. She may be incapable of answering or unlocking the door."

"What should I do?"

His mouth curved in a smile. "I'm an expert lock pick, remember?" He stood and walked to a nightstand by the bed. Reaching into the top drawer, he withdrew a small, black leather case. His eyes caught and held hers. "You must be calm when we open the door. She needs you."

She jumped to her feet. "Of course."

They left his room and hurried down the long hall to the cousins' shared chambers. Glancing both ways to ensure they were unobserved, he withdrew a thin metal rod from the case and inserted it into the lock. Seconds later the door opened.

She started to run inside, but Robert grasped her arm and shook his head.

Despite the tight knots in her stomach, she forced herself to take a deep breath before slowly approaching the bed. Jane was lying on her back, her eyes open but unfocused on the ceiling, her body completely still. For a heart-pounding moment, Sophia wondered if her cousin was dead until she spotted the slight rising and falling of her chest.

"Jane, it's me. It's Sophia."

No response.

Robert stepped forward and reached for Jane's hand. Sophia watched as he pressed two fingers on the inside of her wrist. She realized he was checking Jane's pulse in the same way a surgeon had once examined her father.

Jane blinked and turned her head to look at Robert, hovering above her. "Please do not fuss over me, my lord. I'm fine. Just tired."

She struggled to sit. He took her arm and assisted her. "I suggest you do not stand just yet, Lady Stanwell."

She nodded woodenly, and then to Sophia's dismay, tears welled in her eyes and rolled down her cheeks.

Robert sat beside Jane on the edge of the mattress and placed an arm around her shoulders. She began to weep aloud, yielding to compulsive sobs that shook her frame, and rested her head on his shoulder. He gently rubbed her back.

Sophia gaped, uncomfortable with Jane's outburst and at a loss as to how to help her. Robert, on the other hand, did not shrink away from the tears. Reaching into his pocket with his free hand, he retrieved a handkerchief and offered it to her.

His comforting ministrations shocked her. Never had she suspected the professional, calculating spy could show such empathy. He had not known Jane long. To the contrary, Jane's sole purpose had been to serve as a proper chaperone for Sophia during the house party.

Yet here he was, patiently soothing Jane like a father would his little girl.

Sophia studied Robert's chiseled profile. She felt a strange comfort as he took charge with quiet assurance. He was proving to be a complex man—a fascinating enigma that she felt compelled to unravel.

Who was the real Robert Ware?

For long minutes no one spoke, while Jane sobbed. Eventually she ceased crying and loudly blew her nose in his handkerchief.

"I apologize," she said. "I never thought of myself as a

weepy woman."

"There's no need to apologize, Lady Stanwell. You've been through a traumatic event," he said.

Sophia moved close. "I'm so sorry you had to experience that…that farce."

Jane glanced at her with red, swollen eyes. Her expression was one of wretchedness, and her voice trembled. "It wasn't a farce. How do you explain the table? The precise description of Charles? Right down to his preferred attire?"

Sophia shook her head. "I don't know, but there must be a logical explanation for—"

"I can help with that," Robert said, drawing the women's attention to him.

"What do you mean?" Sophia asked.

"There is no such thing as a medium. Viscountess Delmont is no exception."

"Do you have proof?" Jane asked.

"I do," he said.

"Please show me, my lord," Jane said.

Robert stood. "It requires a short trip. I can take you now while the rest of the party is occupied in the drawing room playing cards. Are you feeling well enough?" He looked into Jane's eyes. Sophia had the distinct impression he was checking to see if her pupils were focused.

Jane nodded. "Yes, a change of scenery may do me good."

He held out his hand and helped her struggle to her feet.

She visibly trembled, and Sophia noted her face was pale as carved marble—just as it had been during the séance. She was about to voice her concerns when Robert spoke up.

"We can do this later," he suggested.

Jane shook her head. "No. This can't wait. I'm exhausted from the grief of losing my spouse. Can you understand, my lord?" she asked in a low, tormented voice.

Robert hesitated, and a flicker of indefinable emotion passed over his face before he hid it with a polite smile.

What had she seen? Sorrow? Loneliness?

Or was it a quirk of the candlelight in the dim room?

"I will take you. Lean on my arm," he instructed.

He escorted the women down the hall, and they descended the grand staircase. Sophia thought he would turn right and head to the round room where the séance had been conducted, but to her surprise, he led them out the front door instead.

It was a warm May evening, the stars luminous against a curtain of black. A crescent moon cast a soft light over the marble statues around the fountain. Bobbing lanterns illuminated the main footpath leading down to the boxwood hedges and distant maze.

Robert took one of the lanterns and led them away from the main stone path to the dim back gardens. Here the ground sloped down and the white stone facade of the original manor home gave way to the newer polished stone of the addition.

He stopped and studied a small casement in the stone wall. "This is where the séance took place."

"You intend to enter from outside?" Sophia asked. "There is no access from the gardens, and the window is too small to climb through."

"So it would appear. But there is access to the room." He dug the toe of his boot into the grass they stood upon. "Here."

"There's nothing there," Sophia said.

Bending down, he dug his fingers into the grass and pulled back a perfectly cut, rectangular patch of lawn to expose a wooden door with a wrought-iron handle.

Surprise spiraled through Sophia. "A trap door?"

He pulled on the handle. The door squeaked on its hinges and opened to reveal a narrow wooden ladder. She could see only the first few rungs. The rest plunged downward into darkness.

"Where does the ladder lead?" Jane asked.

"To an underground tunnel and a hidden chamber beneath the room," Robert said. "It's similar to a root cellar, but much smaller. A wooden pike is connected to the center of the round table you occupied. I suspect a servant manipulated the pike during Lady Vivian's communications to simulate a disturbance by the spirits."

Sophia's skin crawled as she gazed down the trap door. It would almost be like being buried alive. She had never been afraid of small, dark spaces, but the endless blackness below made her hesitate.

Jane grasped her skirts and crouched down. "I want to see for myself."

"Wait! Is it safe?" Sophia asked.

"I can take you both." Robert turned to Jane. "Are you certain you feel up to this?"

Jane's face was no longer pale, but high with color. Her eyes flashed with determination and passion. "Absolutely."

"I'll go first with the lamp to check if it's clear, then return to assist you. If you spot anyone, leave immediately and head back to the house." There was a lethal calmness in his eyes that made Sophia shudder.

He was gone before she could respond. Looking down,

she followed the light from the lantern. The yellow glow flared into the darkness until it faded and then disappeared completely.

The women remained silent. Sophia's heart seemed to batter against her ears, until minutes later, Robert's voice echoed from below.

"It's empty. I'm coming for you both."

She heard the scrape of his boots on the wooden ladder. His head emerged a moment later. "Who's first?"

Jane put her foot on the first rung.

"Careful, now. The ladder is steep. Go down backward," he instructed.

Sophia followed after Jane. Her heart pounded, and sweat trickled between her breasts. She descended the ladder and stepped onto a dirt floor. The lantern's glow revealed a narrow walled corridor. The air was musty, the space cool and damp, and dust mites swirled in lamplight. Skittering sounds through rotting leaves made gooseflesh rise on her arms.

Rats! She clutched her skirts with sweaty palms.

"Follow me," he instructed. "The tunnel leads to the chamber."

They walked single file through the narrow tunnel. Sophia followed directly behind Robert, his air of calm and self-confidence keeping her anxiety at bay.

"How much farther?" she asked, her voice strained.

"We're almost there," he said.

The tunnel turned right, then a slight left, and then opened to a round chamber. The smell of damp earth remained, but nonetheless, she felt an immense relief as they stepped out of the constricting tunnel and into the chamber. Robert hung the lantern on a hook in the wall, and Sophia scanned the space. Just as he had described, a pike hung from the center of the ceiling.

He grasped the freestanding handle. "Someone was down here during your séance who shook the table and made it tremble and helped the viscountess communicate with her spirits. There are also small holes all around the ceiling." He picked up a bellows resting in the corner and inserted the end into one of the holes. "Air can be blown above, making the participants feel as if ghosts are swirling around them. The entire séance was just as Sophia said—a farce."

"I don't believe it! I was taken for a fool," Jane said.

Robert's eyes were like bits of stone. "From what Sophia told me, you were not the only one fooled tonight. Whoever put the Earl of Stanwell's name in the hat had ulterior motives."

"That's just it. Neither of us has any idea," Jane said.

Sophia's tone was harsh. "The viscountess is coldhearted to use such chicanery."

"I'm not convinced she knows of this room," he said.

Both women stared at him. "What do you mean?"

"Her husband may be responsible. Vivian has always been peculiar. Delmont may be humoring her to keep her out of his business affairs."

"You're jesting," Jane said.

"From what I've seen and heard, she truly believes to have contact with the world of spirits," Robert said.

"She's crazed," Sophia said.

Robert shrugged. "Perhaps." He turned to the tunnel. "Come. We must leave before our absence is questioned."

They retraced their steps and climbed the ladder. Cool night air filled Sophia's lungs. She breathed deeply as Robert shut the trap door and concealed it with the grass.

Once back in the main part of the gardens, Jane turned to him.

"I don't know how you learned of it, my lord, but I am eternally in your debt," she said.

Robert's eyes were contemplative. "Stop blaming yourself for your husband's deeds, Lady Stanwell. Life is too short to perpetually punish yourself. You are not responsible."

Jane's dark eyes shone bright in the pale light of the moon. "You're right, my lord. I vow that tomorrow will be a new day." She curtsied. "If you will excuse me, I'm quite exhausted and will retire for the night. You need not worry, however, I promise not to lock my cousin out."

A corner of his mouth pulled into a smile, and he bowed.

Sophia was both surprised at his tone and thrilled by his words of advice. She had tried to tell Jane before, but she had been unable to help. After what Robert had shown them this evening—combined with the force of conviction behind his statement—would Jane finally be able to put the past behind her?

Sophia looked to Robert as if he could answer her question. He watched Jane depart, an intense but secret expression on his face that heightened Sophia's curiosity about him even more.

He had gone out of his way tonight. He had unlocked the bedroom door, had held and comforted her cousin, had discovered the trap door and taken them down the tunnel and shown them that the séance had been nothing but a well-orchestrated hoax. She could not have done any of those things. She was beginning to see him in a different light. Deep down, he was not the scheming, sly spy that he worked so hard to portray.

She was honest enough with herself to admit that she'd always been attracted to him, but his physical attributes were not what drew her now.

There was more to him…much more that enthralled and lured her. Her scientific mind wanted to learn the truth—wanted to unravel the layers of isolation and aloofness that shrouded him.

Chapter Fifteen

Robert watched as Jane entered the house. Sophia's cousin must be reeling from her discovery for her to absently leave Sophia unchaperoned with him in the front gardens.

He turned his attention to Sophia. Her gaze was riveted on the front door where Jane had entered. A shaft of moonlight illuminated the burnished-copper tresses in her chestnut hair and the shimmer of her blue silk gown, which accentuated her slender waist and the flare of her hips. She looked fragile and ethereal beneath the moonlight, yet he knew she possessed an iron determination.

A will so different from Gwendolyn's.

A disturbing part of him acknowledged that her strength did not lessen her femininity.

Or her desirableness.

She bit her bottom lip — a nervous habit he now recognized when she had something troubling on her mind.

"What is it?" he asked.

She motioned him close to the fountain. A slight breeze stirred loose tendrils of hair across her cheeks, and a fine spray of water glistened at her smooth nape. Glancing both ways, she lowered her voice, and he strained to hear above the sound of running water.

"There's more to tonight's events than I mentioned," she said. "When Vivian was describing Charles's 'presence,' she went into detail about his appearance and his clothing. She spoke of a pocket watch and a dangling fob of gold. It sounded like one of the gold gears."

His gaze sharpened. "Wendover never mentioned that a gold gear was found on the body of the Earl of Stanwell."

"Maybe Charles wasn't wearing his pocket watch at the time of his death. Maybe it's among his possessions."

She made a valid point. He considered how best to discern the truth. "Are you comfortable enough with Jane to ask whether her husband was part of a select group in the Society or if he owned a gold gear without arousing her suspicions?"

She raised her chin, her green eyes flashing with conviction. "I can."

"Good. Keep me informed. Meanwhile, you need to return to the house."

She took an abrupt step toward him. "Wait! How did you know about the door to the tunnel?"

He hesitated and looked at her intently. "Whenever I am on a job I always conduct a search of the grounds. In my line of work, preparation is the key to survival."

Her eyes widened. He suspected she was recalling their mad flight through the gardens the night of the masquerade party. She had been brave that night, just as tonight. He knew she didn't want to climb down the ladder into the underground chamber, but he grudgingly admired her for conquering her fear.

Would anything stifle her spirit?

"Did you tell Jane the truth tonight?" she asked.

"I did."

"You truly do not believe Vivian knows about the existence of that chamber?"

He shook his head. "Like I said before, she seems convinced of her 'talents.' I suspect she has no idea of her husband's underhanded dealings with a secret group."

"Then how do you explain the viscountess's description of the gold gear?"

"Charles was part of the Inventors' Society. She must have seen him on numerous occasions and was able to describe his dress and the watch fob. If she knew what the gold gear stood for, she wouldn't have spoken of it."

"You're right. I should have thought of that."

"You should return before you are missed," he said sternly.

"I must thank you first."

The heady fragrance of the garden's rosebushes mingled with her perfume. She stood less than an arm's distance away from him—a desirable women dangling before him like a piece of forbidden fruit. Reaching out, he brushed away a smudge of dirt on the tip of her nose from the underground tunnel.

She lowered her lashes and stared at his mouth. He felt the inevitable stirrings of arousal.

Christ! He knew better than to touch her. He kept his lust tightly leashed, like the beast it was, but the slightest contact with her threatened his iron control. He mustn't allow his defenses to crack. His current assignment—no matter that it took place at a luxurious house party—was like all the others in that a momentary lapse in judgment could result in deadly consequences.

Finish the job quickly and get her out of your life, his inner voice warned.

She continued, oblivious to his heightened senses. "I wouldn't have been able to help Jane without you."

Grinding his teeth, he fought for restraint. "Do not credit me too much," he said, his tone caustic.

"Don't be ridiculous." She touched his sleeve, her green eyes imploring.

He inhaled sharply at the contact, bringing her scent fully into his nostrils. She was looking up at him with wonder and gratitude.

And burgeoning desire.

He could see it, feel it, taste it—all his senses were fully alive and alert to her.

Her pulse beat wildly at her throat, and her breasts rose and fell above her tight bodice.

Desire blasted through him. One finger…just one finger in the low-cut bodice and he could free the mounds to his eyes, feast on her flesh like the starving man he was. She would be all soft, feminine curves and womanly skin.

So different from the sole indiscretion he had succumbed to in the past.

In the two years since Gwendolyn's death, he had suffered from a rare moment of weakness—one episode where he had given into his base needs. He'd been caught alone in Covent Garden with a demimonde by his friend, Daniel Forster. Even though his friends had believed him celibate, Daniel had respected his privacy and had never spoken of it to their mutual friend, Gareth Ramsey, who often mocked Robert for his choices.

But Robert had been filled with self-loathing.

He mentally shook himself. Sophia was pure—too good to be tainted by the demons raging inside him.

She stepped closer. His heart thundered in his chest, and his arousal throbbed in his trousers. In one smooth motion, she could be in his arms, her body pressed tightly to his.

His voice was harsh. "No, don't—"

"You opened the bedchamber door, you proved the séance a fraud, you—"

"It was in my interest to help Jane," he snapped. "She is your chaperone for the week. Without her presence, you would have to leave, and my orders were clear. Wendover wants me to keep you in line, remember?"

She tilted her head, exposing the ivory smoothness of her neck. "Don't do that. It won't work with me any longer."

"What?"

"You're not as coldhearted or as dispassionate as you want me to believe. The way you comforted Jane was wonderful. Beneath the surface, you're kind and compassionate."

Kind? Compassionate? No one who truly knew him would believe such lies. He had stolen, tortured…killed. Not all his victims had been guilty. His soul was eternally damned.

Yet she was gazing up at him like he was *worthy*. Not just for his appearance—which he knew attracted women—but for his essence, for what lay beneath the surface and deeply buried under layers of guilt and self-incrimination. A spark of long-forgotten need flared inside him. He struggled with the consuming emotion, fought against it. Then her slender palm touched his chest above his pounding heart, and *she* reached up on tiptoe and kissed *him*.

Like a man without will, he pulled her into his arms and kissed her back. Unlike the first time, there was nothing soft about his possession of her mouth. He was burning with need…need to stop her from digging deeper into his soul and need to taste her.

He drew the softness of her bottom lip into his mouth and sucked the tender flesh. Her lips trembled open with an eagerness that made his overheated senses spin. At the first stroke of his tongue, she moaned softly. He angled his head and fit his mouth harder, deeper against hers.

His hands roamed down her back to the curve of her hips, then lower still. He cupped her bottom and pressed her against his hardness. She gasped and arched closer, nestling her soft thighs against him. His arousal strained, pulsed with the pounding of his heart.

He lifted his head. Unmistakable passion burned in her eyes.

"Sophia," he rasped.

"Yes," she breathed.

He gazed down at her, at her green, catlike eyes, her moist swollen lips, and the rounded tops of her full breasts straining against her bodice.

Damn Wendover for forcing her upon him.

"I can't do this," he said roughly. "You have to go back to the house."

He turned and headed for the stables and the escape he desperately needed—a hard ride to calm his harsh breathing and the lust pounding through his veins.

Chapter Sixteen

By the fourth day of the house party, Sophia realized she was making little progress with the women. She decided to change tactics and familiarize herself with the gentlemen. An anatomist was expected to give a group demonstration and lecture that morning, and the viscountess had extended an invitation to the women. Sophia had been quick to accept as it offered the perfect opportunity to converse with the men.

Although Viscount Delmont continued to shoot her furtive glances at every opportunity, she had not been alone with him since the first night she had encountered him in the hallway. She assumed Robert had been searching the house at night looking for clues, but she hadn't had a chance to speak with him alone since the evening they had been together in the gardens.

Memories of their shared kiss lingered in her mind. She had wanted to kiss him, had wanted the kiss to continue, she realized. Her body had been aflame, and from what she could discern, so had his. But he had been the one to pull back.

She had come to the conclusion that there was much more to the Earl of Kirkland than he wanted her to believe. He wanted her to think him cool and aloof, the consummate spy. He used words to insult and inflame, but she was no longer fooled.

Dressing quickly in a morning gown of pale pink with a gathered bodice and muslin overskirt, she rushed down the hall to the landing.

Jane met her at the bottom of the staircase.

"Am I late?" Sophia asked.

Jane shook her head. "The guests are gathering in the drawing room and waiting for Mr. Young. I'm told the anatomist is quite popular in London, and he began his career conducting traveling shows."

"Are all the women attending?" Sophia asked.

"Almost all, surprisingly. Lady Cameron was the only one to excuse herself, saying her disposition does not take well to viewing body parts, even if they are not real."

"One of father's friends was a struggling anatomist. He could only afford to pay the modeler and artist to create a model of a human head. He would use pig, sheep, or ox eyes for his shows," Sophia said.

Jane grimaced. "Uh, Sophia! You really were raised quite unorthodoxly."

Sophia chuckled, once again enjoying Jane's company. Her cousin had been surprisingly calm since the evening of the séance. She had faced the women at breakfast with her chin held high and a devil-may-care attitude that dared any of the ladies to ask questions. None had raised the subject.

Sophia had wanted to ask her whether Charles had owned a gold gear, but the horror of what had happened to Jane lingered. The last thing she desired was to upset Jane's current happiness, and she prayed Jane had taken Robert's words to heart.

The men were already waiting when the ladies entered the drawing room.

She spotted Robert leaning against a curio cabinet, cradling a cup of coffee. Dressed in a buff coat with form-hugging trousers and Hessians, he looked like any wealthy gentleman of leisure who might be found lounging in the bay window of White's or Brooks's. But his well-groomed appearance was incongruous with the power coiled within his lithe frame and the predatory alertness in his gaze.

She wanted to find out which safes he had been able to penetrate and what he'd discovered. The one time she had an opportunity to speak to him, he had appeared uneasy, as if he didn't want to be alone with her. She, on the other hand, wanted to take advantage of their isolation to talk.

She had a burning inquisitiveness to learn more about him and his past. How long had he been a spy? How had he learned to finesse safes open?

Just then Robert met her eyes. His sensuous lips curled in greeting, and he raised his cup.

Sophia nodded and chose an empty seat on the sofa next to Mr. Heinz. Other than Robert, Heinz was the only unmarried man in the house.

"You look lovely this morning, Lady Sophia," Heinz said.

His gray eyes twinkled behind his wire-rimmed spectacles. Despite his scholarly demeanor, he had a full head of brown hair, and she was struck by his youthfulness.

"Do you have an interest in anatomy, Mr. Heinz?"

"My interests are twofold: gunpowder and mechanical devices."

"I understand you own patents for your innovations to the spectroscope and the study of wavelengths of light."

"Yes."

"I have several ideas myself to improve the efficiency of the electric battery."

His interest was obviously piqued. "You invent as well?"

"My father's passion has become mine."

He looked uncertain. "My condolences for the loss of Lord Haverton."

She lowered her gaze to her hands in her lap. "Thank you, Mr. Heinz."

"Please call me Henry," he said, taking her hand in his.

From the corner of her eye, she saw Robert set down his coffee cup on an end table. A swift shadow of anger swept across his face, and his lips thinned.

Heinz's palms were damp as they held her hand. He was clearly nervous. Could she cultivate a friendship and pry him for information? She gently squeezed his fingers and smiled.

"Would you like to see the model of my spectroscope?" Heinz asked.

Raising her lashes, she gazed up at him. "I'd like that very much."

Heinz's eyebrows rose in obvious pleasure. "I will show you later today. I'm told our hosts have given us a few hours off."

He continued to stare at her, his gaze disturbing in its intensity. There was a strange unease about him. He may be comfortable in his workshop surrounded by bits of brass pieces from disassembled spectroscopes, but he was awkward around women. Henry was the cerebral type, not a practiced rogue or charmer.

"Your English is impeccable, Henry. Will you stay in England?" she asked.

"I plan to. My admittance into the Inventors' Society was most surprising."

"In what way?"

"They made me an offer I cannot refuse. Funding for my research and a town house in London."

Interesting. Could Heinz be the newest inductee in the secret group?

"I had no idea the Society had such resources," she said.

Heinz's chest puffed with self-importance. "Viscount Delmont has been most generous. He says my patents are invaluable and I must finish my research. My expenses are of no consequence to him."

She had heard rumors of Vivian's substantial dowry when she had married. Delmont himself was a viscount, but from what her father had said, when Delmont had inherited the title, the estate came with a considerable debt.

So where was the money coming from?

She was stopped from pondering the question when Delmont rose and cleared his throat. "If everyone will be seated, we can begin."

The door opened and a short, middle-aged man with jet-black hair and bushy sideburns wheeled a table the length of a coffin into the room. Resting upon its surface was a wax model of a nude man with a cotton towel draped over its nether parts in consideration of the ladies.

The model was painted to appear extremely lifelike. Its brown eyes were open, and the artist had paid meticulous attention to each facial feature; its eyebrows, eyelashes, nostrils, lips, and earlobes all were rendered in vivid detail. The muscles of its chest and arms were clearly delineated, and a line, which looked like an incision, ran down the center of its breastbone. Two assistants followed behind Young and carried jars of unidentifiable specimens floating in clear liquid.

Mr. Young stopped in the center of the room and waved his arm over the model. "Good morning, ladies and gentlemen. I took the liberty of naming my model John, and his anatomy is scientifically accurate. John is made of a mixture of wax from bees and other insects; other inferior models are made of wood, ivory, or papier-mâché. I also brought along examples of animal anatomy that I will discuss at the end of my lecture."

Young's assistants held up wooden boards with dead squirrels and rodents whose feet were pinned to the board. Several of the ladies shrieked at the sight, but Sophia thought they looked quite pitiful spread-eagled and on display.

Young began his lecture. "The history of anatomy is as old as the history of astronomy. One of the first anatomists was Hippocrates, a Greek physician in the early fourth century before Christ. He was followed by Aristotle, Herophilos, and Erasistratus."

The model was cleverly made, and Mr. Young removed two sides of the chest where the incision appeared to reveal the organs beneath. The heart, lungs, liver, and kidneys were all visible and made of painted wax. When he removed the organs and held them up for the audience to have a better look, both Lady Maxwell and Lady Falk wrinkled their noses and turned away.

Sophia knew anatomists and artists dissected corpses to

create accurate models, and grave robbers were notorious for providing corpses for profit. She wondered what the Delmonts were paying Mr. Young for today's demonstration.

Henry Heinz's eyes brightened with interest at the demonstration. He glanced at her. "I'm relieved to see you do not feel faint."

She smiled at him. "It takes more than a wax model to summon the vapors on my behalf, Henry."

Henry swallowed, his Adam's apple bobbing in his throat. "You're a fascinating woman."

"Yes, she is."

She whirled. Robert stood behind her, his expression thunderous.

Could he possibly be jealous?

Nonsense, her inner voice chided. Robert was playing a role, and he was an exceptional actor.

Heinz swallowed and pushed his glasses farther up the bridge of his nose. "Do you find anatomy interesting, Lord Kirkland?"

"Only Lady Sophia's, not the wax dummy's."

She gasped. Heinz's eyes widened behind his spectacles. What was Robert's game?

The anatomist glanced at them, bristling with indignation that they were speaking during his lecture.

"As I was saying," Young continued. "The heart is the most important organ in the human body." He held up one of the jars. "This is an example of a cow's heart."

Young droned on and on, but Sophia paid little attention. She was tensely aware of Henry Heinz sitting rigid beside her, and Robert towering behind the two of them, his forearm resting on the back of the sofa, his hand inches from her shoulder. She could almost feel the heat from his body brush her shoulder and caress her nape. She glanced up to find Viscount Delmont watching her, his stare burningly intense.

The heat subsided and was replaced with a shiver.

...

Robert was a fool. He knew Sophia was in a better position to elicit information from certain gentleman during the week than he was. She was a beautiful woman who could easily flirt with a man and cajole him to reveal his secrets.

In the course of his career for the Home Office, he had observed female spies. They were essential when it came to espionage and a well-trained female spy was highly competent. They could use tactics he could not. Feminine wiles were invaluable in the art of war. He should take advantage of Sophia's willingness to aid in the investigation and glean valuable information from the men. It had never bothered him to use a woman before.

But Sophia?

He didn't like it. Not just because they were playing a role, and he was expected to act jealous of any male attention toward his future wife. No, there was more to it than that. His role had little to do with the primal rage he felt when another man touched her.

He cursed himself. He'd resented when Viscount Delmont paid her attention the first time he saw her. Even now, the blackguard stared at her from across the room.

Henry Heinz was no different. He was looking at her like a lovesick schoolboy.

Young's voice began to grate on Robert's nerves. "The

liver is the only organ that can regenerate itself…"

Robert shifted restlessly. His fingers itched to twine in Sophia's hair. She was clearly nervous; her breathing was rapid, and her breasts rose and fell temptingly against the low neckline of her gown. He longed to bury his face in her cleavage, wrap himself in her scent.

Young cleared his throat. "The heart is comprised of four distinct chambers…"

How much time before the long-winded anatomist finished? Before he could drag Sophia out of the drawing room and lecture her? She was supposed to talk to the women, dammit, not the men.

Perhaps his frustration wasn't just of a sexual nature. He had broken into three additional safes over the course of the three nights, but found nothing of significance except banknotes, the viscountess's jewels, and a blank sheet of paper that held no hidden message. No leads other than the list of names and the gear he had discovered in Delmont's study safe the first night. No hint as to the identity of a mastermind.

Only Wendover's initial theory that the Inventors' Society was stealing inventions of a military nature appeared to be accurate.

Robert had sent a note to Wendover to look into the money trail. Based on the contents of Delmont's safes and the extravagance of his home, Delmont seemed to have no shortage of money. Robert was certain if they dug into the viscount's finances, they would find the kernel of evidence they needed. If the investigation wasn't concluded by the end of the week, he would follow up in London. As to what he would do with Sophia upon returning to town, he wasn't yet certain.

At last, Young stopped speaking and invited the guests to approach his model and ask questions.

Robert straightened, intending to grasp Sophia's elbow and pull her away from Henry Heinz's presence and out of the room.

Just then Lady Delmont stepped into his path. He watched in frustration as the viscountess ushered the women out of the room for a game of lawn bowls.

He would have to wait for his reckoning. Meanwhile, he had work to do.

...

While the men remained occupied by the anatomist, Robert slipped out of the drawing room and down the hall toward the study. It was a bold move during the day with the servants about, but he had learned long ago never to ignore his instincts and he had a nagging suspicion that something of importance had transpired over the past few days.

Closing and locking the study door, he pushed the sofa aside and rolled back the Oriental carpet to reveal the floor safe. This was the third time he would open the recessed Barron lock.

He had the feel of the lock now, and it took him less than half the time to manipulate and raise the levers. Opening the safe, he glanced inside.

The list remained.

The gold gear was gone.

Just as he'd suspected. Another member had been inducted into the secret group. With only three days remaining of the house party, time was running out.

Chapter Seventeen

Sophia was playing bowls on the expansive lawn when she spotted Henry Heinz making his way back to the house. She suspected he was returning from a brief walk to change for a hunt that the viscount had planned for the men.

Just then a heated argument began between Lady Falk and Lady Maxwell over whose bowl had come closest to the smaller white "jack." Sophia took advantage of the distraction to slip away and return to the house.

Taking the grand staircase to the second floor, she hurried down the corridor. It was before luncheon and if she was spotted by servants or guests, it would appear as if she was returning to her room to rest.

She rushed past her chamber and slipped into a cleaning closet at the end of the hall. She left the door open a crack, and a pie wedge of light lit the small space. A mop, bucket, and broom were crammed to the side. The strong odor of linseed oil filled the air.

Soon after, Henry ascended the stairs and strode down the hall. Opening his bedchamber door, he disappeared inside.

She forced herself to remain still. The closet air was stale and warm and a rivulet of perspiration formed between her breasts in her tight bodice.

Her efforts were rewarded twenty minutes later when Henry left his room wearing brown trousers and a moss-colored hunting jacket. Whistling, he made his way to the landing at the top of the stairs. Only after he descended and she heard the front door slam closed did she step out of the closet.

Quickly making her way to his room, she opened the door and slipped inside. The cloying scent of a cheroot and strong cologne lingered. The maid had not yet entered his room, and a jacket, cravat, and stockings were haphazardly tossed upon the bed and across an armchair.

She removed her gloves and tucked them into a pocket of her gown. After hurrying to a chest of drawers, she searched each drawer for a document, a gold gear, anything that would indicate his affiliation with Lord Delmont, the mastermind, or the secret group.

She ran her fingers along the inside edges of the drawers, feeling for a hidden crevice or nook out of place. Her pulse raced and her breath rushed in and out of her lungs. She pushed loose tendrils of her hair away from her face and brushed a film of perspiration from her brow. Every minute counted. At any moment a maid or Henry himself could walk through the door.

She moved to the wardrobe, then the nightstand.

Nothing.

The mantle clock chimed, reminding her of the time. Nervousness made her gut clench tight.

Spying takes nerves of steel, she thought. *How does Robert accomplish what he does with the safes?*

In a last-ditch attempt, she thrust her hands beneath the mattress hoping to find some evidence.

The tips of her fingers grazed an object. Not metallic, but paper. She fell to her knees and reached as far as she could beneath the mattress until her fingers wrapped around a bundle. Pulling it out, she stared at a stack of banknotes.

English banknotes, not German.

More money from the viscount?

It wasn't unusual for a gentleman to carry banknotes. But Henry Heinz was not titled and she thought he was in need of funds. She made a mental note to convey the information to Robert.

She carefully replaced the banknotes beneath the mattress and rose. Opening the door several inches, she looked both ways before emerging from the room. She closed the door behind her and attempted to steady the wild beating of her heart. Another minute and she would be safely in her own—

A hand clamped down upon her shoulder.

Whirling around, she stared up into Delmont's stony face.

"Well, well…what have we here?"

Her eyes widened. Her hand flew to her chest where her heart hammered erratically against her palm. "My lord! You startled me."

The viscount's eyes darkened like volcanic glass. "What are you doing leaving Mr. Heinz's chambers?"

Her mind panicked at her precarious position, and a

swiftly spreading sense of dread skated along her nerves. Her thoughts were jumbled, and she struggled with a quick response. "Mr. Heinz was kind enough to offer to demonstrate his new spectroscope for me."

"So you sought him out alone in his bedroom?"

She stifled a thick swallow in her throat. "He'd mentioned he was returning to rest."

"You're mistaken. He's hunting with the men."

"Yes, I realize my mistake," she said quickly. "I'll just be on my way." She made to move past him, but he shifted to block her path. His massive chest loomed before her.

Her eyes flew to his. "It was a misunderstanding, my lord."

His rapier-like gaze raked her figure. "If I didn't know any better, Lady Sophia, I'd say your interest in me your first night here was feigned. Regardless of my efforts, I find you elusive."

A cold shiver spread over her as she remembered her father. Her parent had suffered and perished at this man's orders. Despite the fact that they stood in the center of the hall and any shout would easily send a bevy of servants running, her skin crawled and the hair on her nape stood on end.

"I apologize if I've misled you, my lord. I'm engaged to Lord Kirkland," she said.

"Ah, yes, Lord Kirkland. What would he say if I told him of your surreptitious activities?"

She wasn't certain if she should act outraged or acquiescent. She opened her mouth to argue. "I'd hardly call scientific curiosity a surreptitious activity."

"I wonder. Were you truly interested in Mr. Heinz's invention, or were you searching his belongings?" he said.

"I don't know what you're referring to—"

Footsteps sounded down the hall.

"There you are, Sophia. I've been searching all over for you."

She spun at the familiar masculine voice to see Robert approach.

Thank the Lord! she thought.

Robert was smiling, strolling lazily…almost cockily down the hall before stopping before her and Delmont. Dressed in an unbuttoned navy jacket, loosely tied cravat, and buff-colored trousers, he appeared like any at-ease country guest, fully enjoying the festivities and everything their host had to offer.

She wasn't fooled. Beneath the polished veneer, he was all lean muscle and coiled power, and she had never been as happy to see him. She prayed her relief wasn't obvious to Delmont.

"It's time for our garden stroll, my love. You do remember, don't you?" Robert said, his tone light.

She was quick to catch on. "Of course, I remember."

"Good. I don't want to leave Lady Stanwell waiting. She's agreed to escort us." Robert winked at Delmont. "I'm sure you can understand why I'm passing on the hunt."

The viscount nodded tersely, remaining silent.

Robert steered her away and down the corridor. Once they turned the corner, his pace changed and quickened. Priceless landscapes hanging on the walls whirled by in a myriad of color. They rushed down the stairs, and the heels of his Hessians clicked on the marble vestibule. She hurried to keep up with his brisk pace as he escorted her out of the front door.

Glancing at his profile, she saw he was no longer the relaxed suitor come to take her for a garden stroll. She was struck by his serious expression, his narrowed eyes, and the muscle that ticked at his jaw.

He was angry, furious.

He followed the stone path into the well-kept gardens, and she dragged a breath of air into her lungs. His grip on her arm was like a vise, pulling her along beside him.

"Stop," she said.

His voice was like finely sharpened steel. "Not yet. Into the maze."

Chapter Eighteen

Having little choice, Sophia followed Robert into the immaculately trimmed maze. Once they were deep in the shrubbery, he halted beside a stone bench and turned on her.

"First Delmont, then Heinz. What are you up to?" he asked.

"I'm trying to discern the truth."

His eyes narrowed. "Delmont mistrusts you now. Any scrutiny on his part can reflect upon me. It could compromise the mission."

Her chin jutted out defiantly. "I'm sorry. Since you tell me little, I thought to find out more on my own."

"You're playing a dangerous game, madam."

"Then tell me more, let me in." At his silence, she prodded, "I won't stop. I will keep asking questions."

An emotion flashed across his features before he hid it with a sardonic smile. What had she seen? Admiration? Irritation?

He ran his fingers through his hair, pulling it away from his scalp. She watched, fascinated by the multihued color as the strands threaded through his fingers.

"All right," he muttered. "I'll tell you everything I have discovered so far. I've searched most of the safes in this pile of stone and have found nothing but banknotes and the viscountess's jewelry. Other than the list of names I discovered the first night in the study, there is nothing that hints at who the mastermind is, what the gold gears stand for, or what the secret group is up to."

"Are we back to the beginning then?" she asked.

"Not entirely. The last gold gear is gone and I suspect another inventor has been inducted into the group."

She bit her bottom lip. "It has to be Henry."

"It's Henry now, is it?"

She ignored his sarcasm. "Mr. Heinz told me that he is staying in London and all his expenses will be paid by the viscount courtesy of the Inventors' Society."

He whistled through his teeth. "Heinz is a likely candidate. His fast-burning gunpowder should bring a good profit on the black market."

"I've thought the same thing," she said.

"There are other members who are not present at the house party. I suspect Delmont is paying their way in town as well."

"How?"

"The members pay dues; however, they are not sufficient to cover living expenses. Research costs even more money. I sent a missive to Wendover requesting a search of Delmont's finances. It seems the man has plenty of blunt, but his sources of income remain a mystery."

"I wondered that as well after speaking with Mr. Heinz," she said. "I searched his room but found nothing incriminating, only a few English pounds stuffed beneath his mattress."

The tick at his jaw returned. "That was foolish and dangerous. What if he returned and discovered you?"

"He didn't.

"You should have told me of your plans."

"I knew you wouldn't approve."

"You are the most maddening woman I have ever met."

"Thank you."

"That wasn't a compliment."

"It was to me." She met his hard gaze. "I want to be a full partner, not just someone to whom you give a spattering of information when you deem it necessary."

Several heartbeats passed. "I've come to the conclusion that you're right."

"You have?" She had expected a fight, not his agreement.

"Yes. You should be involved in safer aspects of the investigation."

"Such as?" She wasn't sure this was much of an improvement. She was already assigned to speak with the women.

"Aspects that I cannot do. Such as talk to Mr. Heinz to see whatever information he may unwittingly reveal to you. However, you must only do so when you advise me in advance that you will engage him, and you must never again conduct a clandestine search without my knowledge. In return, I will continue to keep you apprised of all that I discover."

"I see. And what about Viscount Delmont?" she asked. "Should I encourage his attentions and try to learn more from him?"

His tone was hard. "No. That issue is not negotiable."

She decided not to push him or her luck. He was agreeing to keep her informed and let her take a more active role. At least he recognized that she could glean more information from a bachelor like Henry Heinz than he ever could.

"All right," she agreed.

He nodded curtly. "Since we are both in agreement that Mr. Heinz is most likely the newest member of the secret group, we need to look at him more closely. See if you can encourage him to keep talking."

"How?"

"He's clearly enamored. Under normal circumstances, I would advise any female spy to use that to her advantage."

"I fully intend to—"

He steeled his jaw. "But not you. I don't like it."

"You don't?"

The iris-blue hue of his eyes sharpened. "I despise the idea of any man touching you, gazing upon you with ill-disguised lust."

"Why? Because we are supposed to act the loving couple?"

"No. Because it makes my gut clench and my blood pound and because I want to beat any admirer to a bloody pulp."

Her breath caught. "Oh, my."

She couldn't think of anything else to say so she simply reached out and touched his cheek. He was warm...warm and hard and...heaven help her, deliciously enticing.

"You have tested my patience like none other," he said, his voice harsh.

"I know." Her hand remained, cradling his cheek.

And she felt the slight tremble in him.

The tremble that revealed more to her about him than his medievally possessive words. He desperately needed human contact, was starving for it like a thirsty man traveling through a long, desolate stretch of desert. He was isolated, alone. Without the caring touch of another for so long, his need strained in every sinew of his body. There was no question: something had happened to him…something cataclysmic and devastating.

But how far would he let her go?

"What happened to you?" she asked.

His gaze sharpened. Became cautious.

Undaunted, she traced her finger down his chiseled jaw to the cleft in his chin that had fascinated her the first time she'd seen him at Delmont's masquerade ball.

He grasped her ungloved hand, but didn't push her away. Rather he pressed his lips to her palm.

Her breath hitched at the touch of those perfect lips on her skin.

"I tried, dammit. I tried to warn you…tried to warn myself to steer clear," he muttered.

"Why?"

He lowered her hand, but didn't release her fingers. "I'll end up hurting you."

"You're not going to hurt me. I'm a grown woman, and I can look after myself. I trust you."

"No. Don't say that."

"I do. I trust you."

"I'm a bloody fool." His head lowered an inch, his breath fanning her lips.

She tilted her face toward him, and her lashes fluttered, every nerve ending tingling…waiting, wanting, craving his kiss.

He hesitated; her eyes opened.

I want this, she thought. *I desperately want him to kiss me.*

She rose on tiptoe and closed the distance.

At the first touch of their lips, a yearning growl rumbled deep within his chest. He drew her tight against him, and his kiss was like the soldering heat that joined metals. She felt her knees weaken and her fear and inhibitions melt away. It didn't matter that they were in the center of a garden maze in broad daylight with the sun streaming down upon her upturned face. The threat of discovery only heightened the forbidden…the excitement. There was a strange bond between them, as if he had been waiting for her to heal him and she had been waiting for him to show her the mysteries of pleasure.

He cupped her buttocks and pulled her against him, holding her tight against his hardness and letting her know of his desire. Liquid heat pooled low in her belly and between her legs.

Her hands slipped beneath his jacket and roamed the muscles of his shoulders and back. She felt a rope-like scar through his shirt, and she had an overwhelming urge to remove the barrier of his clothing and study every inch of his flesh.

He carried her to the stone bench and sat, sweeping her onto his lap. His lips recaptured hers, more demanding this time, while one hand cupped her breast. Then his finger slipped inside the bodice of her silk gown to graze her nipple, and the sensitive peak instantly grew taut from his touch. Pleasure radiated outward, sending currents of desire through her.

He whispered against her lips, "Sophia…I was right. You'll drive me mad. You're untouched and deserve better."

In response she arched her back, eagerly inviting him. She was vaguely aware of him working the fastenings at the back of her gown. The silk gaped away, and he tugged at the low neckline exposing her shift. He cupped one soft mound, then returned to kissing her, until her senses whirled from his lips and his touch. His lips trailed a path down her throat to her breast, and he kissed and licked her nipple through the thin cotton.

Gasping from the pleasure, she looked down as he laved her breasts. Her swollen nipples stood out through the wet garment. She felt no shame, only the exquisite feelings flooding her limbs.

"You're so passionate. So beautiful."

She felt beautiful. He kissed her again. Melting kisses. Slow, shivery kisses. She squirmed in his lap, rubbing against his hardness. Lifting the hem of her skirt, he let his hand travel up her calf and past her silk stockings and frilly garters to caress her thigh. His fingers found the slit in her drawers and brushed the silken curls between her legs. She inhaled sharply when he found her most sensitive woman's flesh. He stroked the bud slowly, skillfully, until she was wet with need and her body quivered from his slightest touch.

"I want to kiss you here," he murmured.

She was shocked. Could a man do that to a woman?

She clutched his arms. "I'm so hot, Robert. Is it always this way?"

He lifted his head and the passion in his sapphire eyes was startling in its intensity. "God, yes. Hot. Wet. Let me show you what it can be like for you."

She wasn't ignorant of how humans mated. Her father's library had been full of scientific books and treatises. But none had mentioned the rioting emotions, the delicious sensations coursing through her body. This was different. *He* was different. And she wanted to experience more.

"Yes. Show me," she breathed.

She was urgent in her need. He held the key to some indescribable release. It was a purely sensual experience, and her heartbeat throbbed in her ears. He touched secret places she didn't know existed, and she surrendered completely to his masterful touch.

His tongue thrust into her mouth, matching the rhythm of his fingers. She grew desperate, clawing his shoulders, returning his kisses with wild abandon until a sudden cry tore from her. Her body tightened like a bow and a sharp release pushed her beyond the precipice, leaving her clinging to him.

She looked up at him through half-closed lids. His eyes were shut. His body tense. Perspiration beaded on his brow. He didn't look like a rogue or a womanizer, but a man riven with need.

With sudden certainty, she knew that she wanted him. Wanted all of him. She had no illusions. The fact that he was a government agent, a man who could never offer a commitment— whether through marriage or with his heart—did not deter her.

She was twenty-four years old and had come to the conclusion long ago that she would not marry. She'd never been interested in carnal passion, only the intellectual passion she'd felt while working on her inventions in her workshop. No men had drawn her, not Henry Heinz or any of the gentlemen she had danced with at the many fancy balls she'd attended. Only Robert, with his thin veneer of respectability, made her feel weak with longing. He alone drew her like a lodestone and was impossible to resist.

With shaky hands, she reached for the closure of his trousers.

"Wait." His eyes flew opened, and he grasped her wrist.

She looked up at him. "I want to touch you, too. Please, let me."

He groaned low in his throat. "God, yes."

He was a man of nimble and agile fingers, able to finesse open the most complex mechanical locks, yet he was unable to accomplish the simple task of unbuttoning his trousers.

Pushing his hands aside, she pulled his shirt free of his waistband. She glimpsed the sprinkling of crisp hair on his chest that trailed downward to the muscular ridges of his abdomen, and lower still...to the prominent bulge in his trousers. She reached for the buttons and flicked them open. The fabric parted to reveal his manhood.

Heavens!

Once again, books had not adequately prepared her. A shiver of fear rippled down her spine at the size and length of him. Eyes wide and heart pounding, she reached out and touched him. He was like smooth iron—hot and hard—a fascinating, erotic contradiction.

How could he fit inside her?

Then he groaned again and all her apprehension fled. She touched the vermillion tip and a pearl of liquid lubricated her hand. She ran her fingers down his length and he moaned with pleasure. Encouraged she wrapped her fingers around him.

He jerked and hissed.

She pulled back. "Am I hurting you?"

"No…no. It's just been too long."

Too long? A man like him would have flocks of women eager to bed him, yet all her instincts cried out otherwise. His response told her otherwise.

She met his hot gaze. "I want to be with you."

"No. Not with me. I can never marry."

"Good. I don't want to marry."

"I'm not worthy, Sophia."

"Stop. Don't speak that way."

He shook his head. "Not here. Not now."

"Then let me please you."

"Yesss."

He showed her how to hold him, and she watched as he began to pump in her hand. His hips rose and fell, and she was fascinated by his muscles straining and his masculine beauty. With knowledge as old as Eve, she knew she held great power over him. He closed his eyes, threw back his head. The corded muscles of his neck strained against the loose cravat. She sensed he was close to his own release…

Feminine voices sounded over the high hedge. A trill of laughter followed.

His eyes snapped open. She was struck by the raw, desperate need in the blue depths.

Oh, Robert. What happened to you?

He jumped to his feet and quickly righted his clothing. He then whirled her around and started with the tiny row of buttons at the back of her gown.

The voices sounded closer. A sense of urgency passed between them. They both understood the consequences if they were found alone and half-dressed in each other's arms.

Once her buttons were refastened, she spun to face him.

"This isn't over. We need to talk about what happened," he said.

We need to talk about you. "I—"

He cut her short, pointing to the pathway leading out of the maze. "Go before we are discovered," he said in a tense, clipped tone. "I'll remain behind and distract them."

This time she didn't argue and turned and fled.

Chapter Nineteen

Robert watched Sophia go, his hands fisted at his sides. He counted to ten, then breathed in through his nose and out through his mouth. Sexual desire ravaged against the urge to protect and possess. His need was greater than it had ever been in his life.

More so than with Gwendolyn.

Not for the first time he questioned his fierce attraction to Sophia Merrill. She had the same effect on him that she'd had the first time he'd kissed her: instant, combustible lust. He could not control his hunger for her any more than he could cut off a limb.

The thought barely crossed his mind before another formed. She wasn't a first year debutante, but a mature woman who desired him. Why couldn't he?

His resounding answer was dredged from a place beyond logic and reason, but nonetheless undeniable. He wanted Sophia with a desperation bordering on obsession.

To hell with Henry Heinz, Viscount Delmont, or any other who desired her. The only man who would touch her, kiss her, was himself.

He'd have to move on after the mission was concluded; there could be no future between them. Even with his new title, he would never consider himself proper husband material. Not when his life involved the daily dangers of espionage. He'd learned that brutal lesson long ago with Gwendolyn.

Yet somehow his motives had changed. The simple had become complex. To entrap Delmont and the mastermind for certain, but also to claim Sophia and protect her from the unseen dangers the mission would undoubtedly reveal.

...

As Sophia hurried back to the house, her body still hummed with delight from Robert's skillful touch. Erotic images of what had transpired in the gardens filtered through her mind. Her heart thumped erratically as she recalled his passionate kisses, the strength and warmth of his flesh, and the earth-shattering climax she'd experienced before they had been interrupted.

She had longed to touch him, to kiss and stroke his magnificent body until he reached his own fulfillment. Yet she sensed that his need was deeper than a sexual release, and she'd never forget the low growl that had rumbled from within his chest from her simple touch.

But how could he be a stranger to women? To human contact?

He'd wanted to talk about what happened between

them. She wanted to talk about *him*. More specifically, his past. But how could she bring up the subject?

She made it to her room and changed into a dress of pale primrose muslin embroidered with tiny roses. By the time she finished and closed her bedroom door, she was late for luncheon. Her slippers were silent on the Oriental carpet runner.

At the sound of angry voices in the corridor, she slowed. *What in the world?*

The shouting was coming from the Brass's assigned rooms. She halted and glanced about. The hall was empty; the guests had long ago headed for the dining room. Ducking behind a large, ornate Chinese vase on a pedestal and pressing her back against the plaster wall, she strained to hear.

"I cannot believe you put the Earl of Stanwell's name in the hat for the séance. Lady Stanwell must have been distraught. That was above cruel, even for you, Emma." Mr. Brass's voice.

"I told you I didn't do it to be cruel. I thought it would add to the entertainment. I never believed the viscountess a real medium or the séance would work!"

Sophia stood stunned by the admission. Emma had put Charles's name in the hat as a joke? Sophia's temper flared at the thought of what Jane had suffered. It took all of her self-control not to burst into the room and strike the silly woman.

The couple continued arguing, and she remained in her spot, more intent on eavesdropping.

"We shall leave this place. I'm finished with the Society," Mr. Brass said tersely.

"You cannot be serious, George. You're finally a member. How can you think of leaving?" Emma asked.

"I've made my decision."

"An opportunity like this comes along once in a lifetime. Think of the money we can earn with their influence. You will have the funds to pursue your inventions. The ton *will visit your shop, and I will receive invitations to all the Season's soirees."*

"Is that all that concerns you? Money? The beau monde*?"*

"Am I so different than your first wife—"

"That will be enough!"

Just then, the bedroom door opened and Emma burst out, slamming the door behind her. Her skirts whirled around her ankles as she rushed down the corridor and down the stairs.

Sophia remained frozen against the wall, thankful the other woman hadn't noticed her. She prayed the Brass's bedchamber door would remain closed so that she could discretely pass. The last thing she desired was to be a witness to the couple's domestic quarrel.

Grasping her skirts and stepping from behind the Chinese vase, she attempted to hurry past just as the door swung open and Mr. Brass stepped out.

He halted upon spotting her and cleared his throat. "Lady Sophia, I apologize for that display. Mrs. Brass has quite a temper."

Sophia stood awkwardly. "I was just passing by. There's no need to apologize."

Mr. Brass shut his bedchamber door and stepped toward her. "Are you on your way to luncheon?"

"I am."

He offered her his elbow. "May I escort you?"

How awkward. Yet how could she refuse him? Manners dictated that she accept. She placed her hand on his sleeve. "That would be lovely."

Mr. Brass led her to the landing and down the grand staircase. "I couldn't help but overhear from Lady Stanwell that you are an inventor."

"My father's workshop has become mine, and I hope to follow in his footsteps," she said.

"I wasn't aware women were allowed in the Inventors' Society."

"They're not."

"It's for the best." They passed the vestibule and soon entered the maze of corridors that led to the dining room.

She tilted her head to the side and regarded him. "Are you suggesting women are not intelligent or creative enough to become inventors?"

Mr. Brass chuckled. "Others may hold that opinion, but not me."

"Then why is it for the best that I not join?"

He leaned close and looked at her from beneath craggy brows. "If it was up to me, I wouldn't have joined myself."

"It's certainly not required," she pointed out.

He drew his lips in thoughtfully. "Maybe not to others, but Mrs. Brass is—how can I phrase it—ambitious."

"She forced you to join?"

"I have no opposition to what the Inventors' Society stands for."

"Then what?"

He sighed wearily. "I'm old and no longer need validation in my life for my achievements. Personal satisfaction comes from within, not from a fancy society. I'm also a simple jeweler and engraver—an artist at heart—but Emma is young and wants to be more than the wife of a shopkeeper, no matter how successful my business grows."

Not for the first time, Sophia wondered why Mr. Brass had married an overly ambitious woman less than half his age. "You must be true to yourself," she said.

He hesitated and appeared to be in deep thought. "Did I ever tell you that I knew your father?"

Her step faltered. "No."

"He helped me once. When I began my business years ago, he came to me to buy a piece of jewelry. A locket."

She looked up at him stunned. Reaching for the filigree chain around her neck, she pulled out her locket. "This?"

"Yes."

She flicked the heart-shaped piece open to reveal a tiny portrait of a middle-aged man. "It has a picture of my father. He gave it to me when I was a young girl. I've worn it since."

"He purchased it from my first shop and requested I engrave it with a specific message from father to daughter. At the time my shop wasn't doing well, and he offered to lend me money until business improved. If it wasn't for him, I would not have succeeded. I paid him back years ago and we parted ways, but I never forgot his kindness. The Marquess of Haverton was a good man."

She swallowed the lump in her throat. "I had no idea. Father never mentioned it to me."

"I'm not surprised. He was a true gentleman."

They had reached the entrance to the dining room. Most of the guests were already seated inside.

"Take care, Mr. Brass." She placed a quick kiss on his cheek before entering the dining room and heading for her assigned seat.

Chapter Twenty

Robert had decided to skip luncheon and had sought a quiet place to think. He'd discovered the billiard room vacant and had just finished racking the ivory balls when the door opened and Gareth Ramsey stepped inside.

"What the hell are you doing here?" Robert asked.

Gareth strode forward. "Is that any way to greet a friend?"

His broad, towering frame had intimidated many opponents in the boxing ring and in the courtroom. But the two were good friends and it took more than bulk to intimidate Robert.

Gareth picked up a cue stick and joined him at the billiard table. Robert watched him shoot a ball into a side pocket.

"I find it hard to believe you've yearned for my company for the short time I've been away. So why are you here?" Robert asked.

"I received an urgent missive from Mr. George Brass requesting a consultation," Gareth said.

"Brass is recently married to a much younger lady. Don't tell me he's seeking your services already?"

"I met with the man earlier. He tells me his young wife is difficult to live with. He realizes a divorce is impossible and seeks an annulment or legal separation."

A flurry of movement outside the window caught Robert's eye. A group of women strolled past on the garden path. Sophia was amongst them. Her face was flushed, her eyes a brilliant emerald. She walked arm in arm with Jane, laughing.

"Is the smiling brunette Lady Sophia?"

"It is."

"Ever since I met her at Lord Cameron's ball, I've been meaning to compliment you. She's certainly not an eyesore."

Robert scowled. "I never said she was."

"Considering your staunch celibacy, I never thought you intended to marry."

"I don't, remember?"

"Ah, yes. Wendover ordered the betrothal."

"That's right."

"Even though you're just following orders, I still have hope that the lady can pull you out of your celibacy," Gareth taunted.

After years of secrecy, Robert longed to share the truth with him. But where to start? That he had secretly married Gwendolyn? Or that he had accidently murdered his wife and his celibacy was a form of self-punishment.

Robert set his cue stick down on the edge of the billiard table, but before he could speak, Gareth interrupted.

"What do you know about Lady Sophia's cousin?"

Robert's brow furrowed at the question, and he looked

at Gareth.

But Gareth's attention was once again riveted out the window, his dark eyes intently studying the women. Robert realized he'd been worrying for naught. Gareth had no interest in questioning him further about his feelings for Sophia. His friend's thoughts were clearly preoccupied elsewhere.

"Lady Stanwell is a widow," Robert said. "Her husband shot himself, supposedly over a gaming debt."

Gareth turned away from the window, his eyes narrowed. "Supposedly?"

"Some believe she drove him to commit suicide."

"Bollocks."

"I agree. Society is malicious." Robert began to line up the ivory balls on the green, felt table. "Why the interest in Jane? You prefer courtesans. She doesn't strike me as a woman who would dally in a casual affair."

"You're wrong about that," Gareth drawled. "My gut tells me there's fire beneath her widow's weeds."

Robert stared. "You find her a challenge?"

Gareth shrugged. "She's a beautiful woman."

Robert chuckled. "Careful, Gareth. Else *you* just may find yourself caught in the marriage trap."

Robert laughed at Gareth's taut expression. Then his thoughts turned and he contemplated telling Gareth about his current mission. The Home Office frowned upon an agent sharing information about an ongoing mission with others, but Wendover also stressed an agent should do what was expedient. Robert was no closer to incriminating Delmont and knew Gareth's presence could help.

"I'm glad you're here," Robert said. "I'd like to make the

best of the next few days."

"I understand Viscount Delmont keeps his guests well entertained."

"That's not what I had in mind. I can use your help for the remainder of the week."

Gareth's eyebrows rose inquiringly. "You have my interest."

"Tell me, what do you think about George Brass?

Gareth shrugged. "He's an old man who made a mistake with his choice of spouse."

"How about Viscount Delmont?"

"I don't know him well enough. His wife appears to be a bit peculiar, but warmly welcomed me to stay for the remainder of the house party. Why?"

"The viscount and several of his fellow inventors are up to something," Robert said.

"Illegal?"

"Yes, but I don't know in what capacity yet. Wendover suspects Delmont is working for a mastermind who is killing off inventors and selling their inventions for profit. There is evidence of a secret group within the Society. I need you to keep your ears and eyes open for me," Robert said.

"Does Lady Sophia know?" Gareth asked.

"She suspects. But only three days remain of the house party, and I need to make the most of them."

Gareth slapped Robert on the back. "You can count on me."

"There's something you should know about me," Robert said. "Daniel already knows."

Gareth's mouth quirked with humor. "That magpie knows something I don't?"

Robert struggled to maintain an even, conciliatory tone. "I know that you believe me uninterested in the fair sex lately, but the truth is I was married to Gwendolyn."

"You're jesting?"

"No."

Gareth's amusement swiftly faded. "Why not tell me? Why the secrecy?"

"I blame myself for her death."

"Don't be ridiculous. She died in a riding accident. You talk like you murdered her."

If you only knew, Robert thought.

"There's no need to be secretive," Gareth said. "If you prefer to keep it quiet, then I'll never speak of it. As for Delmont, I'll do what I can to keep watch."

Robert nodded. "Good. How about we ring for one of the viscount's countless footmen, request a bottle of his fine whiskey, and discuss strategy?"

...

Late that night, Sophia tossed in bed unable to sleep. The viscountess had kept the women busy during the day with an outdoor walk of the vast grounds followed by games of whist in the drawing room after dinner. Robert had been noticeably absent all evening.

She fluffed her pillow in frustration, trying to find a more comfortable sleeping position, when a scraping sound at the door alerted her.

She sat up bewildered. Her eyes focused in the dim light, and she turned to see Jane in the nearby four-poster. A shaft of moonlight from the window illuminated the bed, and the sheer silk canopy had been pushed aside. Her cousin lay unmoving and for several seconds, Sophia watched her chest rise and fall and listened to her soft snore.

Quietly rising, she went to the door and found a piece of paper that had been slid beneath the crack. She picked up the sheet and tiptoed to the window. Moonlight cast light upon the bold, black script.

> *Lady Sophia,*
>
> *Kindly meet me in the conservatory at half past two. I have something of your father's. He'd want you to have it.*
>
> *Mr. Brass*

She frowned. The nature of the note was mysterious, but the content fascinated her.

She fingered her locket. She'd worn the necklace since she was a child, and she had been surprised to learn that Brass had made the delicate piece and engraved the message. Whatever he had, she wanted as a memory of her father. Perhaps it would reveal something about his death.

Yet she wasn't a fool. Why the mysterious note in the middle of the night? Was he afraid of his wife's disapproval? She recalled the Brass's fight and wondered just how strong a hold Emma Brass had on her elderly husband.

She clenched the note in her hand. She had promised to keep Robert appraised of all her actions. Reaching for her wrapper, she quietly opened the door and set off to find him.

• • •

Robert turned onto his side in bed. He had spent the

remainder of the evening with Gareth drinking, playing billiards, and strategizing about the mission. They'd discussed the secret group, Viscount Delmont, and where else Robert could search for clues.

He had avoided talk of Sophia, but he knew Gareth suspected more when it came to his relationship with her. As a shrewd, experienced barrister, Gareth was trained to observe human behavior.

If he wasn't distracted by Jane, he would have questioned me further. I must be prepared for his inquiry.

Robert shifted onto his back. The manor was silent; all the guests had retired long ago. An owl hooted in a tree close by his window.

He dreamed he was back outside DeForte's house and waiting for the Comte's fine carriage. His breath was visible in the frigid December air as he crouched behind the bushes. His spyglass was focused on the front door. The guards had rotated. The Comte's carriage slowly traveled up the stone drive.

DeForte stepped out, followed by Gwendolyn.

But why was his wife with the traitor?

The question had haunted him for over a year after Gwendolyn's death until he'd discovered the truth.

The scenes unfolded in a different order as he tossed…

The answer had been in the safe of another Englishman, an assistant to the prime minister. Robert had climbed a trellis and broke a casement lock and lowered himself into the man's bedroom.

He had found the incriminating documents at the bottom of the safe: a list of names of agents working on behalf of England against Napoleon's tyranny. Robert's name was third on the list. Beside each agent's name their family members were identified in neat block print. Several had been crossed off.

So was Gwendolyn's.

A suffocating fury encompassed him. His heart pounded with the force of a mallet.

The dream changed...

He was standing in Wendover's elegantly appointed office, his face set in stone as he handed his superior the list.

"Napoleon's agents have unearthed ours," the marquess said. "They sought to hunt you down and torture you until you revealed everything, but you proved elusive. DeForte sent a missive to Gwendolyn saying you were in trouble. They must have planned to use Gwendolyn as bait to lure you into a trap. They didn't know you had already been assigned to assassinate DeForte and infiltrate his house that fateful day."

Robert thought of Gwendolyn's beliefs. He took deep breaths, unclenched his fists, and tried to calm his racing heart.

What would she have wanted? What would she have told me?

The words were the hardest he'd ever voiced out loud. "I want out."

"Out?" Wendover said incredulously. "I'd think you'd want revenge."

"DeForte is dead," Robert said.

"What of the cause? The threat of Napoleon's invasion of England and the lives of our countrymen?"

"There are others that can fight the fight without me."

"I understood why you wanted to retire after marrying

Gwendolyn, but now that she is gone, I'd have thought you'd want to stay in espionage," Wendover said.

"You thought wrong."

"Can I change your mind?"

"No."

Robert woke with a pounding headache. He was cold, shivering, yet sweat covered his entire body. His bedcovers were twisted about his legs, and he kicked them off. Panting, he cradled his aching head in his hands and sat on the edge of the bed.

He had indeed left espionage, left working for Wendover and the Home Office. He'd returned only when one of his father's closest friends and his wife had been threatened by a madman.

When Wendover had contacted him, Robert had agreed to take care of the matter. Looking back, he'd known the price: he'd remain working for the Home Office.

The most frightening fact of all, he realized, was that he'd missed it. The theft, lying, cheating, and murder...it was a part of him—a part he needed in order to feel alive, a part as deeply embedded as the marrow in his bones.

Until now.

The throbbing in his temples built in intensity. He was having doubts again—doubts that had nothing to do with his past marriage or the lies he told his friends, but with his growing obsession for Sophia. More and more, she invaded his thoughts. At a time he should be concentrating on the mission, he was thinking of how the cut of her gown emphasized her full breasts and her long legs. How good she smelled...and tasted.

Worse still, how he *felt* when he was with her.

He was thinking irrationally. The assignment would eventually end—they always did—and he would part ways with Sophia Merrill. She'd call off the betrothal. The scandal would pass, and she'd go on with her life and marry a rich, titled lord and bear him many heirs.

Bloody hell.

He rose and splashed water from a basin onto his face. Cold rivulets ran down his chest and wet his shirtfront. He breathed in deeply and exhaled. Rubbed the back of his head.

It was no use. He felt as if the four walls of his chamber were closing in and the air was stifling. He needed the cold night air to cool his blood and ease the pounding at the base of his skull.

After donning riding boots, he left the room and headed for the stables.

Chapter Twenty-One

Sophia rapped softly on Robert's door. "Robert?" she whispered as loud as she dared. No response. She rapped again, slightly louder, and waited a full minute. She couldn't imagine that he was such a sound sleeper. The man was trained to hear a mouse's steps upon a carpeted floor.

She opened the door cautiously and looked inside.

The coverlet and sheets were on the floor in a twisted heap. Robert was gone.

A quick glance at the mantle clock told her it was already half past two. Dare she wait longer?

No, Mr. Brass might give up and leave, and she desperately wanted to learn what he knew and claim her father's items.

She moved quickly to an escritoire and scrawled a note for Robert explaining the summons and where she was going. Then she set off for the conservatory.

It was eerily quiet as she crept down the stairs and through the winding hallways holding a single candle to light her way. She came to the conservatory, opened the door, and stepped inside.

It was dim, save for a sliver of moonlight through the parted curtains. The light from her candle illuminated a nearby pianoforte and a Roman bust resting upon a marble pedestal. In the far corner, a group of music stands cast shadows like stalking cats upon the ceiling. She felt a prickle of uneasiness.

"Mr. Brass?"

Silence.

"I received your note. It's Sophia."

She walked forward slowly, holding the candlestick in front of her. She tripped over something and caught herself before she stumbled.

A low moan pierced the room. Gooseflesh rose on her arm. "Mr. Brass, is that you?"

Another moan. She lowered the light to see George Brass lying on his back. His eyes were closed and blood trickled down his forehead, soaking the Oriental carpet.

"Mr. Brass!"

Kneeling beside him, she touched his brow. His flesh was cool, his breathing shallow. She spotted it then—the silver figurine of a shepherdess on the carpet beside his head. Without thinking, she picked it up and recoiled at the blood on its base.

"Sweet Lord," she whispered vehemently.

Just then, she heard voices in the hall.

"Something's amiss, I tell you. Mr. Brass always retires before me, and I'm concerned. I heard a noise down the hall."

"Are you certain, Emma? I heard nothing."

Sophia recognized the first voice as belonging to Emma

Brass. The second was the viscountess's.

Panic rioted within her. She couldn't be found here. At any moment the women would stumble upon the scene. There was blood on her hands, and she was alone in the middle of the night with an injured man. She hastily wiped her hands on her wrapper and immediately realized she'd made a mistake. Blood smeared the white cotton, making it look like she had savagely attacked Brass.

She stood and hurried to the door, intending to flee to her bedroom and lock herself inside.

The conservatory door swung open, and Robert stood in the doorway.

"I received your note. You shouldn't have gone," he said tersely.

She shook so badly she feared her knees would buckle. Her voice wavered. "He's…he's been attacked."

"Who?"

She pointed to the body. "Mr. Brass. He wanted me to meet him here…in the conservatory. He was a friend of my father's…and he wanted to give me something…something of his."

"You were set up."

"By whom?"

"Delmont, no doubt. He wants you disposed of. What better way than to have you arrested for murder?"

She shivered.

He crouched by Mr. Brass and sought his pulse. "He's alive, but his pulse is weak. Whoever did this left him to die."

Voices sounded outside, closer now. *"We have yet to look in the conservatory. Perhaps he headed there,"* the viscountess said.

Anxiety spurted through her. "We're trapped! There's

no other way back to our rooms than through the corridor."

Robert strode to the window, broke the casement lock, and thrust it open. On his way back to her, he knocked over the Roman bust.

"What are you doing?"

"Saving you."

Grasping her hand, he dragged her out of the conservatory to the room directly across the hall.

"Inside. Quick."

She rushed to obey. He closed the door behind her, and she found herself in the billiard room. Two rectangular billiard tables occupied the center of the room and cue racks were mounted on the walls.

Seconds later earsplitting screams sounded across the hall.

"We'll look guilty!" she said.

"No, we won't."

Stepping close, he spun her around and tugged her arms from the bloody wrapper. He wadded it in a ball and shoved it under the settee. Loosening his cravat, he shrugged out of his jacket and then tore the bodice of her nightgown, rending the delicate fabric from her neck to the tops of her breasts.

"Act passionate," he commanded.

He pulled her into his arms and scraped the stubble on his chin across the exposed swell of her breasts above her bodice. Bending her backward over a billiard table, he stepped between her legs and jerked her nightgown up to her thighs.

The door was thrown open.

A high-pitched female voice pierced the air. "What in the world!"

Robert straightened; Sophia remained trapped between

his hard thighs.

He cleared his throat. "My lady, we were just—"

"I see what you are doing." The viscountess's voice was shrill. "Mr. Brass has been attacked across the hall in the conservatory."

His brow furrowed. "Attacked?"

"Did you two see anything?" Vivian asked.

"I'm afraid we were occupied."

He took a step back; Sophia straightened and clutched her torn bodice to her breasts. She did not have to feign the blush that stained her cheeks.

Emma Brass continued shrieking across the hall, and within minutes the entire household came running. One by one the doorway of the billiard room became crowded. Men and women in dressing gowns and wrappers hovered in the hall.

Viscount Delmont pushed his way through the crowd. "Mr. Brass took a nasty hit to the head. And you two saw and heard nothing?"

Robert stepped in front of Sophia. "Nothing."

"No wonder. It appears they couldn't wait for the altar," Lady Falk drawled, censure dripping from her voice. She shot Jane a cold look. "Your services as chaperone are clearly lacking, Lady Stanwell."

Jane appeared in the doorway. She frowned, obviously confused by it all.

Delmont looked from Robert to Sophia, and she felt impaled by his dark gaze. "Summon the constable along with the surgeon!" he commanded the closest servant as he strode out of the room.

Chapter Twenty-Two

The surgeon was first to arrive. Mr. Brass was carried upstairs by two footmen and a weeping Emma Brass trailed behind them. A half hour later, the constable knocked on the front door.

The guests gathered in the drawing room at the constable's request. Sophia had changed into a demure dress of blue alpaca and sat on a sofa with her hands folded in her lap. Jane sat stiffly beside her, the tension between them thick.

Robert and his friend, Mr. Gareth Ramsey, who Sophia learned had arrived yesterday, stood beside the mantle.

She studied Robert beneath lowered lashes. He appeared as strong and steady as the stone hearth. He had handled the situation with cunning and efficiency—a testament to his experience—and if her reputation was ruined tonight, then such an outcome was much more desirable than going to prison.

The constable, a freshly minted recruit in his early

twenties, carried himself with a cocky air of self-importance. He held a small pad and pencil.

"I'm Constable Miller and I am handling this investigation. I inspected the scene of the crime in the conservatory and it appears that Mr. Brass was struck over the head with this," he said, holding up the silver figurine.

The blood had not been wiped off, and she felt queasy at the sight.

"The casement lock was broken and the window open. Also, a Roman bust was toppled. The evidence leads me to believe Mr. Brass walked in on a burglar."

Viscount Delmont's eyes flashed imperiously. "You believe it was a common burglary?"

"I do. The criminal must have attacked Mr. Brass in order to escape."

The women gasped.

The constable shut his pad. "I'm satisfied it was a common burglar and Mr. Brass was an unfortunate victim." He put his hat on.

The viscount came forward. "I suggest everyone retire for the night. I'll escort the constable out."

The guests shuffled out as a dazed group. Gareth and Jane stayed behind with Robert and Sophia.

Once alone, Jane turned on Robert. "What happened tonight? And don't bother with the same story you just told the constable," she whispered vehemently.

Gareth spoke first. "Not here. The walls have ears."

Jane glared at Gareth. "What do you know about this, Mr. Ramsey?"

"Gareth is privy to anything I say," Robert said. "I suggest we go upstairs."

They proceeded to escort Sophia and Jane to their bedchamber.

Once at their door, Robert glanced both ways to ensure they weren't being observed, and then the men followed the women into the room and shut the door.

Jane's expression was tight with strain as she stared at Robert. "Who are you, Lord Kirkland?"

Robert's expression was grave. "I work for the Home Office. I've been investigating a series of murders of members of the Inventors' Society. A secret group within the Society is suspected of selling inventions of a military nature to foreign militias for profit."

"You're a spy?" Jane asked incredulously.

"Yes," Robert admitted.

Sophia was shocked. She'd thought he would fabricate a story, not reveal his true role.

"And Sophia knows this about you?"

"We've been working together," Sophia said quietly.

Raw hurt glittered in Jane's brown eyes. "How could you not tell me?"

"I didn't want to put you in any danger," Sophia said.

"Is your courtship a sham as well?" Jane asked.

"We were to break off the betrothal after the house party."

"If you're still able," Gareth drawled.

Jane shot Gareth a withering glance before returning her attention to Sophia. "He said the Home Office was looking into a series of murders. Sophia, do you suspect this secret group of murdering your father?"

To Sophia's dismay, tears formed in her eyes. "Yes. Especially Viscount Delmont."

"I'm convinced Delmont tried to frame her for murder tonight—which means he must suspect Sophia of having knowledge of his illegal agenda. What I don't know is why he chose to harm George Brass," Robert said.

"I do." Sophia fingered her filigree chain and locket. "Mr. Brass wanted to leave the Inventors' Society. He knew my father and had made my locket years ago. He wrote me a note requesting that I meet him in the conservatory tonight, but when I arrived he had been attacked."

"Brass didn't send the note," Robert said. "Delmont did."

"So Viscount Delmont attempted to murder Mr. Brass just because he sought to leave the Inventors' Society? It doesn't make sense," Jane said.

"Maybe his wife did it. She could have learned that Mr. Brass sent for me to dissolve their marriage," Gareth said.

"I'm not surprised," Sophia said, turning to look at Jane. "I overheard them arguing. Emma Brass is heartless. She put Charles's name in the hat for the séance."

Jane gasped. "Why?"

"To heighten the entertainment."

Anger flared in Jane's eyes. "Oh, for heavens sake! Has everyone lied to me?"

Guilt pierced Sophia's chest like an arrow. The crippling emotion combined with the night's horrid events was overwhelming and a hot tear trickled down her cheek. "I'm so sorry for keeping any of this from you, Jane. There were many times I wanted to tell you, but I feared for your safety."

Jane was quick to embrace her. "Please don't cry, darling. I understand. In my grief over Charles, I failed you after your father's death. But no longer." Jane glared at Robert. "Lady Falk and Lady Maxwell are notorious gossips and they plan to return to London tomorrow. My cousin's reputation is surely destroyed. Do you intend to act honorably, Lord Kirkland?"

"I do. Pack your bags. We'll leave in the morning. I'll send notice ahead to the priest at St. George's," Robert said.

Sophia stepped out of Jane's arms and wiped her eyes with the backs of her hands. "What are you saying?"

Extraordinary blue eyes blazed in his face. "We're getting married."

...

After the men left, Sophia stood with her back pressed to the door, the shock of Robert's statement reverberating through her mind.

Had he really insisted they marry?

Their relationship had started out as a farce—an engagement of convenience that could not possibly evolve into a real marriage. It was as unfathomable as the man himself.

He was a spy. His intentions had always been clear. He'd never wanted their sham betrothal and he'd never marry. If not for Wendover's insistence, she would have been left behind in London. Their engagement was to last the length of the investigation, not a day more.

And what of the mission? If they departed immediately, Robert would not be able to complete his task. The secret society would not be revealed. Viscount Delmont wouldn't be arrested. Her father's murder would go unpunished.

She was aware of a rustling of covers as Jane sat on her bed.

"This is madness," Sophia whispered.

"Which part? That your engagement was never real or that you've been involved in a secret investigation with a spy?"

"Is it really that bad?"

"It is, considering you were discovered by Lady Delmont sprawled half-naked over a billiard table."

Sophia winced. "Robert never wanted any of this. He attempted to dissuade me and his superior out of the sham engagement."

"Knowing your stubborn streak, I sympathize with Lord Kirkland."

"You don't understand, Jane," Sophia protested. "He's vehemently opposed to marriage."

"He no longer has a choice. Thankfully, he understands the consequences and intends to act honorably."

Sophia swallowed hard, suddenly angry at the turn of events. "I don't want a husband who is forced to marry me just to save his honor or mine!"

"What do you want, Sophia?" Jane asked.

"The truth is I don't want to end up like…like—"

"Like me? Like my marriage with Charles?"

Sophia bit her bottom lip. "What I mean to say is that just because a woman marries does not necessarily guarantee her happiness."

She had watched Jane suffer from Charles's neglect. If Robert was forced to the altar, would she suffer the same fate?

Jane's voice rose an octave. "Do not think for one moment that Lord Kirkland is similar to Charles."

"I do not want to be a burden as a wife. I want to be a partner," Sophia insisted.

"I've seen the way you look at each other. Is marriage to Lord Kirkland that inconceivable to you?"

No, her inner voice cried out. Robert was unlike any man she knew, and she feared she was falling in love with him. There was kindness, honor, and compassion in him. She'd witnessed all firsthand. And there was an undeniable magnetism between them. He had but to look at her, and she felt a breathless surge of excitement. Time together had not diminished her infatuation. Each time she saw him, the pull was stronger and more enticing.

But there were dangerous secrets in the depth of his turquoise eyes, too.

Frightening secrets. Darkness and cruelty.

"I trust him, but there is a side to him I don't know. I may never know. How can I marry a man with such secrets?"

Jane rose and held Sophia's hand. "Despite what I said to Lord Kirkland tonight, you must know that your happiness is more important to me than any scandal. We could travel to Scotland where I have distant relatives. We need never set foot in England again. But you must be sure that you do not want him. He's prepared to do right by you, and I believe deep down he is a good man, an honorable man. Are you certain?"

"Yes. No. I don't know."

"Then allow me to be a horrid chaperone for the second time tonight. Go to him. Talk to him. Be certain. For if we remain tomorrow you may not have a choice."

Chapter Twenty-Three

Robert poured himself a glass of whiskey and set the decanter down on the nightstand by his bed, an arm's length away. Leaning back on the oak headboard of the four-poster in his room, he let out a long held in breath.

After leaving the women, he had stealthily retrieved Sophia's bloodstained wrapper from beneath the billiard room settee and returned to his bedchamber. He'd dispose of the evidence on their way to London.

He drained his glass and poured himself another. He was tired but suspected sleep would elude him for the remainder of the night. His blood had yet to calm. His rioting emotions had nothing to do with Brass's attack, or their near escape from the constable, but from the danger posed to Sophia.

He should be grateful she'd at least left him a note telling him of her plans to meet Brass, but he was too angry at the risk she'd taken. And when he'd opened the conservatory door and found her covered in blood…

He'd known fear…true fear unlike any he'd experienced before; the stress of a hundred prior missions had paled in comparison. For a fleeting instant he'd thought her injured.

She could have died and left me just like—

His gut clenched tight, and he took another swallow of the whiskey.

Within seconds of observing the scene, instinct and training had taken over. He'd acted quickly to stop Delmont's malicious plans to frame Sophia for a violent crime.

But he hadn't been able to prevent complete disaster.

She had been found half-naked in his arms, ready to be ravished. Her reputation was destroyed; they'd have to marry at once.

The thought should shock him to the core. Repulse him. Frighten him. It didn't.

Instead he'd known a possessive fury at the thought of her harmed in any way tonight. The unnerving truth was undeniable: Viscount Delmont and the mastermind suspected Sophia. The blackguards deemed her a threat to the secret group, and therefore, they wanted her eliminated.

The stakes had clearly risen. Sophia's safety…her very life hung in the balance. They must not be given a second chance to harm her.

He'd told Jane that he would marry Sophia. He had every intention of carrying out that statement, but unlike Jane, he wasn't solely concerned with Sophia's reputation. As an unmarried lady without her father's protection, Sophia was an easy victim. He'd be in a better position to keep her safe as his wife.

He would be breaking his vow never to remarry. But he'd broken his own vows before and had suffered the consequences. This time, he would be saving an innocent woman's life.

He'd have to stay emotionally distant. He understood himself enough to know that this would require every ounce of his strength and resolve. Sophia tempted him at all levels—intellectually and sensually.

He closed his eyes and let the alcohol ease his tension. The house was quiet as all the guests had retired for the second time that night. He focused on his breathing—in and out—and concentrated on relaxing.

Images flashed through his mind, blinding in speed as the dream returned. He was on his knees in the bushes outside DeForte's house.

The fuse was set. Check.

The explosives in place. Check.

The rotation of the guards. Check.

The Comte's carriage slowly rambled up the stone drive and came to a stop before the enormous country house. The door opened and DeForte stepped out. Robert's breath caught. He waited for the first sight of Gwendolyn. A dainty slipper appeared on the lowered step, a voluminous pink gown followed. A woman stepped down.

Chestnut hair, not blond.

Taller and curvaceous, not petite and slender. His mind struggled to comprehend.

Sophia! What is she doing here?

He knew to expect the explosion, but nonetheless it caught him off guard. A flying roof slate cut his temple, and blood oozed into his eye. His ears rang as if he had stood inches away from a tolling church bell. He opened his mouth to scream, but his lungs filled with smoke and the stench of burning flesh singed his nostrils.

Someone firmly grasped his shoulder.

"Robert! Wake up."

Reacting instinctively, he grasped the hand and squeezed. A female whimper pierced his brain.

His eyes sprang open, struggling to focus. "Sophia! What are you doing here?"

"I came to talk. Please…you're hurting me."

He instantly released his grip and sat upright. "Bloody hell! Haven't you heard of knocking?"

"I knocked as loud as I dared without alerting anyone. When you didn't answer, I opened the door. You were tossing in bed and mumbling in your sleep."

He ran a shaky hand down his face. The dream had been frighteningly vivid. Never before had he pictured another victim in place of Gwendolyn. But Gwendolyn hadn't been in DeForte's carriage. It had been Sophia when the fuse had reached the explosives. Sophia who would have been blown to pieces.

"Are you all right?" she asked softly.

He opened his eyes to see the look of concern etched on her face. Her green eyes were large orbs, her full lips slightly parted. She wore the same blue gown she had changed into when they were questioned by the constable, but there were creases in the fabric and tendrils of chestnut hair had escaped the knot at her nape and curled around her neck.

Slowly, she reached out to push a wayward lock from his damp forehead. Despite everything, pure lust blasted through him and he was powerless to quench it.

"You shouldn't be here. What of your cousin?" he said darkly.

"She knows. I came to talk."

"We can talk tomorrow." He swung his legs over the side of the bed and stood.

She shook her head and held her ground. "You were having a nightmare."

Yes, I was. And, in it, I murdered you. Ghostly fingers of the dream still lingered in his mind. He pinched the bridge of his nose, tried to clear the vision. *Get a hold of yourself, man. It was just a dream, damn it.*

He looked at her. She stood proudly before him…vividly alive and alluring. Her delicate perfume teased his nostrils.

"You called out a woman's name," she said hesitantly. "Gwendolyn."

His insides froze. The name sounded entirely wrong on her lips. "Did I?"

"Is there a woman in your life?"

The flash of pain in her emerald eyes was his undoing. For a heart-stopping moment, he wanted, with a desolate loneliness that cut as deep as a well-honed blade, to share his darkest secrets with her. Years of buried guilt and pain wrestled deep in his chest, yearning for release, knowing the compassion in her heart and the comfort of her body would offer a healing salvation for his tortured soul. His tongue felt thick in his mouth as he struggled with the words.

At his prolonged silence she must have assumed the answer to her question was yes. Her painful expression shuttered and was replaced with a look of firm resolve.

"I shall leave with Jane first thing in the morning. We will not return to London. You do not have to act honorably and there doesn't have to be a wedding," she said.

"Sophia—"

"I will tell Lady Delmont that I have cried off from our betrothal. There will be an incredible scandal and I will surely be deemed a jilt, but your reputation will be untarnished."

"Sophia—"

"It will be difficult to walk away before those responsible for my father's murder have been brought to justice, but I trust you to see that Viscount Delmont and the mastermind are arrested for all their foul deeds—"

He grasped her upper arms and shook her. "Sophia, stop."

Her facade cracked, and tears welled in her eyes. "I refuse to come between a love match."

The words came surprisingly easy to him then. "Gwendolyn was my wife. She died two years ago during what was supposed to be my last mission. The explosives I had planted for a treasonous French double agent killed her as well."

She stilled in his arms, and her mouth gaped. "I'm sorry. That must have been devastating."

"It was. I had sworn never to remarry."

"You can keep your vow."

"No. I can't and I won't. Viscount Delmont is a dangerous enemy. I won't let you go unprotected. You're marrying me and that's final."

"Please…you don't have to do this."

He realized that she might still refuse him, and he knew a possessiveness so fierce he acted the only way he knew how. He crushed her to him and claimed her mouth in a searing kiss. His lips were hard and searching, devouring her softness. He expected her to protest, to push away. Instead a brief shiver rippled through her, and she parted her lips and yielded to his dominance as their tongues tangled in urgent abandon. In that instant, the loneliness, the guilt, the pain... all fled on a savage swell of desire that stole his breath.

Desperately wanting more, he unfastened buttons and hooks and pushed the gown down her arms. Her shift was embroidered with tiny flowers, and he traced the petals with his fingertips. She arched her back, and he cupped her full breasts, grazing his thumbs across the thin fabric covering her diamond-hard nipples.

Somewhere in the recesses of his mind, he knew he was dangerously close to ravishing her. He had never wanted a woman as badly as he wanted Sophia, but she was a virgin who deserved to be initiated slowly and gently by her first lover. His skin burned for the heat of her touch, his lust threatening to override reason and restraint.

Drawing upon every remaining thread of his will, he pulled back. Their eyes locked, their ragged breath came in unison.

"Sophia, if you stay I won't be able to stop. You'll be mine."

"I know," she breathed.

"There's the risk of a baby."

"Can you take...measures?"

"There are ways."

"Then make me yours."

The last vestiges of his control shattered.

He growled deep and low. Picking her up, he carried her to the bed and eased himself beside her. He pushed her clothing down to the swell of her hips. He licked one nipple then sucked it into his mouth and eased himself between her legs.

Her fingers kneaded his chest and fumbled with the buttons of his lawn shirt, but his patience had dissipated and he tugged on the buttons and pulled off his own shirt and tossed it to the floor. The feel of her breasts on his skin made him tremble with need.

He worshiped her with his mouth, a series of slow, shivery kisses on her lips, her neck, each of her breasts. All the while his hands worked her gown and shift down her legs until yards of fabric fell to the floor. He made quick work of the drawstring of her drawers and her stockings until they too were tossed aside and she was gloriously naked beneath him.

"Ah, Sophia." He gazed down upon the golden glow of her body in the flickering candlelight. "You are so beautiful."

She reached up and caressed his jaw. "I've always thought you were beautiful. Not just your face, but here," she said, lowering her hand to rest it against his pounding heart.

As he stared into her eyes the hardened shell around his heart cracked open. The world and its troubles tilted on its axis and then melted away until only Sophia existed for him. He was drowning in sexual and possessive need and he could not stop himself from fully marking her, claiming her as his.

He left her long enough to remove his trousers. Her gaze roved down his body and widened as it came to rest upon his hardened manhood. Then she smiled tentatively up at him and opened her arms. He came to her in a rush of desire and captured her lips in a hungry kiss while his hands explored the curve of her hip, her stomach, and lower still.

His fingers grazed her feminine mound, parting the silken curls that shielded her femininity. His breath was ragged as his finger eased inside, testing her. She was blissfully wet, and her throaty sighs and trembling limbs told him that she was ready, but he had an overwhelming need to taste her first, to claim her in every way.

Sliding down her body, he cupped her bottom and raised her core to his mouth. Her musky scent drove him as he flicked his tongue over her sensitive bud. She gasped in surprise, tried to twist away, and grasped fistfuls of his hair. He wouldn't relent and continued to lick and lave her petal-soft skin until her inner thighs quivered and she moaned and writhed beneath him.

His body cried out to sink inside her and ravish her in mindless possession, but he held back, bringing her to the peak of pleasure, holding her there.

Her fingers dug into his shoulders. "Please, Robert. I need..."

He rose above her and eased the tip of his shaft into her slick sheath.

"Robert," she breathed.

He slid inside her slowly until he reached the barrier and then plunged inside in one powerful stroke. He groaned deep in his throat, the pleasure was so pure and explosive. She was so hot and wet, sheathing him like a glove.

She gazed up at him with big green eyes, and his heart ached that he'd caused her pain.

"Are you all right?" he asked hoarsely.

She nodded bravely.

"Wrap your legs around me."

She complied, and he slowly imbedded himself to the hilt. He withdrew and thrust once, kissing her hungrily. Through sheer force of will, he slowly repeated the motion, until she began arching her hips and meeting him halfway. A passionate moan slipped through her lips, and she raked her nails down his back.

All thoughts of going slowly flew from his mind as he breathed in deep, soul-drenching drafts and plunged inside her, their bodies in exquisite, sensual harmony. He wouldn't last, couldn't last, and just as he thought he would explode, her inner walls tightened around him and she cried out in blissful surrender. He withdrew, abandoning himself to the ecstasy, spurting his hot seed across her soft belly.

Chapter Twenty-Four

Sophia awoke slowly, aware of the warmth of Robert's body beside her, the heady scent of lovemaking, and the ticking of the mantle clock. Her limbs felt languid as if she was floating in a warm bath.

He was on his side, his arm around her. He appeared to be sleeping, and she was free to study him at leisure. He looked almost youthful, completely relaxed and without the continuous wariness that she had learned to spot in his gaze. He was skilled at disguising his watchfulness to others, but it was there, hidden in the blue depths of his eyes. Her gaze roamed lower, and she noticed scars on his chest, thin white slashes of puckered skin. She wondered what had caused them.

She had so many questions, but soon the faint light of dawn would peek through the curtains and threaten their temporary sanctuary.

She shifted and eased away, hoping not to wake him.

Muscular arms instantly tightened around her and his eyes opened. "Did you think to escape so easily?"

"Only as far as to my room."

"It's a little too late to fear repercussions from your cousin."

"It's not Jane I fear, but the rest of the household."

He nuzzled her neck, sending a warm shiver through her. "Truly? Or do you have regrets?"

"None. Although, I would like to know more about you."

"Ask and I shall try to answer," he whispered, his breath hot against her ear.

"How did you get these?" she said, tracing the scars on his chest. His skin was warm and damp.

"Each has their own story." He pointed to a thin scar on his right pectoral. "This one was from a particularly stubborn safe door. This one," he said, pointing to the scar on above his right hip, "was from jagged glass as I crawled through a broken window."

"And this?" She touched the three-inch long scar above his heart.

Sadness reflected in his eyes. "That was from a piece of flying brick from the explosion that killed Gwendolyn."

"You blame yourself?"

"I do."

"Why?"

"I'd rather not talk of it." His voice, though quiet, had a tenseness that forbade further questions.

He was retreating behind the all too familiar mask of detached spy and she didn't want that. Not now. Not after what they had just shared.

"How did you become a safecracker?" she said, changing

the topic.

A slight smile tugged at the corners of his mouth. "I was a young Oxford student in need of funds. I saw an ad in the *Times* that was paid for by renowned locksmith Joseph Bramah offering two hundred guineas to anybody who could pick his newest lock."

"Two hundred guineas!"

"Bramah described his new lock as 'Impregnable as the Rock of Gibraltar.' Needless to say, he was overly confident in his invention when issuing the challenge. All manner of people showed up that day, many petty thieves and burglars. And of course, one impoverished university student."

"I take it you were successful?"

"It took me six hours and twenty-seven minutes, but I finally picked the lock and proved it wasn't invincible. What I didn't know was that people other than Joseph Bramah were watching. I was approached by the Marquess of Wendover soon after to work for the Home Office. In my youthful ignorance, I thought spying and safecracking exciting work and wanted to help my country."

"You don't sound so altruistic now."

"I know better."

He stroked her skin from her shoulder down her arm. "My turn to ask questions."

"You know everything about me."

His hand roamed lower to explore the hollows of her back. "Not everything. Tell me about your inventions."

She sighed, distracted by the magical stroke of his hands. How could his touch be so soothing and arousing at once?

"Tell me," he urged.

She struggled to concentrate on his question. "You

know I've been working on completing my father's chemical formula. I fear I'm no closer than he was."

He shook his head. "I don't want to know about your father's work. What are *your* ideas?"

"I've been working to increase the efficiency of the electric battery. I also have prototypes for a self-tying corset and an improvement to the closed, coal-fired stove."

"Fascinating."

"You truly think so?"

"When we return, I plan on applying for your first letters patent."

"You're jesting."

"Why would I be?"

"Father never believed any of my inventions worthy of a patent."

"Then he was wrong."

Her pulse quickened at his words and the touch of his warm skin against hers.

Heavens! Her heart was in trouble.

Her father had never stopped her from tinkering in his workshop as long as she never interfered in his own work. She'd loved him for his unconventional notions when it came to her, but at the same time he had never believed her inventions notable enough to seek a patent. A frown creased her brow as she thought back. He'd mostly ignored her work.

"Why didn't you ever marry, Sophia?"

His question caught her off guard. "A scientific mind is not a desirable one, and an intelligent woman is not a sought-after wife. Men of the *ton* assumed I'd inherited my father's eccentricity, his 'madness.' I had decided not to marry."

He rose on an elbow to gaze down at her. "Then they

are all fools. You are a beautiful woman, but it is your intelligence that sets you apart and draws me."

Perhaps her heart was already lost. It was a slippery slope, a treacherous decline into full-fledged love.

"I'm not the only one to note your intelligence," he said. "I suspect it's why Viscount Delmont attempted to dispose of you tonight. He already knows you have been looking into Henry Heinz, and he doesn't want to take a chance that you will not cease your efforts."

She bit her lip. "What if we never find the evidence we need to have the viscount arrested?"

"I shall. Meanwhile, there can be no reprieve from our vigilance. Delmont is dangerous. I'll feel much better when we are married and back in London. I expect a full report of his financial resources and we can follow up on Sir Falk and Sir Maxwell, the two other suspected members."

"You said 'we.'"

"I want you by my side. I'll waste no time in moving you into my home."

She didn't know what to make of his statement. Once they married, it was understood that she'd reside with him. Still, she couldn't imagine leaving the home she had been born and raised in, the home that housed her workshop. Of course, she had never planned to marry Robert either.

His blue gaze sought hers. "I know what you are thinking, and you need not worry. Ours can be a marriage of convenience. I realize you may not want me after Viscount Delmont and the mastermind are in prison."

"But that's impracticable. We will be married."

"Gareth specializes in matrimonial matters. He can file for an annulment with the courts."

"An annulment? On what grounds?"

"Tonight was magical, Sophia, but I fear I have taken advantage of your innocence. The marriage will never be consummated. You need not tell them about the night *before* your wedding. No one will question an annulment. My friends know me as celibate."

She stared at him in amazement. How could he be celibate? Yet deep down she knew it to be true. She recalled their time together in the gardens when he had said it had been a long time for him. Yet it was the fierce need in his expression, not just of a sexual nature, that had alerted her to much, much more.

She struggled to compose her voice. "You kept away from women after your wife died?"

A flicker of unease darkened his eyes and something more. Something deep and vulnerable.

"I was mostly successful. But that doesn't matter. What matters is that the courts will permit the annulment. You deserve better. A decent man without my dark past. I won't stand in your way. You will be free to live your life."

His words were meant to be reassuring, but she felt anything but comfort. Clearly, he punished himself for his wife's death. But for such a handsome, virile man of his age to refrain from women? A hollowness centered in her chest.

"You'd best return to your room. It's been an eventful evening," he said.

Yes, it had.

"Let me." He retrieved a basin of water from the nightstand and a handkerchief and proceeded to gently bathe her of the evidence of their lovemaking. Then he helped her with the fastenings of her gown. Her hair was beyond repair and she smoothed it back as best as she could.

Placing a brief kiss on her forehead, he cracked the door. "Wear something pretty. We shall make haste to London and head directly for St. George's Church."

She tiptoed silently on the way back to her room, her thoughts flitting through her mind. The evening had been magical for her, and she'd answered truthfully when she said she had no regrets. Most surprisingly of all, he had revealed part of his past, and the tragic story of his wife's fate made her heart ache for him.

She couldn't help but wonder: after the investigation was over, would she want a marriage of convenience to turn into a real marriage?

Chapter Twenty-Five

"I never imagined your wedding breakfast to take place in Claridge's dining room," Jane said.

"Neither did I," Sophia said.

They sat in the hotel's resplendent dining room at a table with a starched gray linen cloth. As soon as Sophia drank her coffee, an attentive waiter refilled her Wedgwood china cup.

The previous morning, they had wasted no time and immediately departed Hatfield. They had stopped at a posting inn for the night and had promptly resumed their journey the next day.

When they had arrived in London early that morning, they went straight to St. George's church in Hanover Square. Robert had sent a missive ahead and the priest was prepared for their arrival. Jane had held Sophia's bouquet of roses, and Gareth had stood beside Robert. The only guest present in the pews was the Marquess of Wendover, who had initially arranged for the reading of the banns. The ceremony was surprisingly quick, and before Sophia could comprehend it all, she and Robert were pronounced husband and wife.

Jane peered at Sophia over the rim of her cup. "Is it too late to ask if you are confident of your decision?"

"It is."

"For a new bride, you look highly troubled and you've spoken less than a handful of words since leaving the church."

Sophia twisted the starched napkin in her lap as she thought of her unexpected marriage and future living arrangements. Her belongings would have to be moved to Robert's home. And what of her workshop? She finally had her own space, and she would have to relinquish it for the time being.

"Lady Falk and Lady Maxwell are troublesome gossip-mongers. They will undoubtedly relish spreading word of your billiard-room antics," Jane said.

Sophia's brows drew downward. "We're married now. Surely the gossip will not last."

Jane shrugged. "The aristocracy loves a scandal, and the Season is far from over."

Oh, dear. She'd survived society's scrutiny when her father was alive. She'd hated every whisper about the "Mad Marquess." Could she live with the vicious gossip again?

It's worth it, she thought. *Everything is worth it if father's murderers pay for their crimes and they never kill an innocent man again.*

She peered at Jane and chose her words carefully. "May I ask you something about Charles?"

"Because it is you, then yes."

"Did Charles own any watch fobs?"

"He possessed dozens. He changed his clothes and accessories more than I did. His valet was constantly in a frenzy."

"I'm referring to one in particular. A round gold fob. Something akin to a gear. It may even be inscribed with a capital letter *I*," Sophia said.

"Why the interest?" Jane asked.

"Robert thinks the gears are a token upon acceptance into the secret group."

Jane took a quick, sharp breath. "You think Charles was a member?"

"I don't know."

Jane lips thinned. "He wasn't. You are welcome to search Charles's belongings. But I am certain about this. Charles was self-absorbed and narcissistic and far too consumed with betting on his precious horses to join and commit to a secret, criminal group."

Sophia nodded. "I believe you."

Suddenly a look of discomfort crossed Jane's face. Abruptly setting down her coffee cup, she focused her gaze over Sophia's shoulder.

Sophia turned in her chair to spot Gareth Ramsey's tall figure enter the dining room. The gentlemen, including the Marquess of Wendover, had previously stepped outside to smoke cheroots. She had assumed they'd needed an excuse to privately discuss the mission.

"What is going on between you and Mr. Ramsey?" Sophia asked.

"Absolutely nothing."

"Don't be ridiculous. You face is beet red."

"Shh. He's spotted us and is coming our way," Jane

whispered urgently.

"Exactly my point."

Gareth approached their table and bowed, his massive shoulders filling the coat he wore. "Ladies, it's been a pleasure, but I must return to my Gray's Inn chambers."

"Thank you for your assistance, Mr. Ramsey," Sophia said.

"Please call me Gareth. I think of Robert as my brother and therefore now consider you a sister." A mocking smile teased his lips as he turned to Jane. "You need not look so dismayed, Lady Stanwell. A sister is the last word I'd use to describe you."

Jane stared as he departed. "The nerve of the man!"

"You're attracted to him," Sophia said in wonder.

Jane's head snapped up. "I most certainly am not! Besides, don't you remember what he does for a living?"

"I do."

"Can you imagine? *Divorce. Legal Separation. Annulment,*" Jane whispered the words as if they were poisonous.

Uneasiness settled in Sophia's chest. Robert had mentioned the last choice as a fate for their own marriage. If she was truthful to herself, his insistence upon a temporary union was as much a reason for her post-marriage nerves as anything else.

The door to the dining room opened once again and Robert stepped inside. His hair was ruffled by the wind, giving him a ruggedness that added to his appeal. Their gazes locked, and he flashed a charming smile. In the shaft of light from a nearby window, he looked like an artist's rendition. Gold highlights gleamed in his tawny hair, and his teeth were white against the bronzed perfection of his face.

Memories of their lovemaking were vivid in her mind, and she recalled the smoldering passion that had thrilled her. She couldn't help but wonder if he would succumb to the desire that had overtaken them both and visit her bedchamber or would it truly be a passionless marriage of convenience? Was their one night together to be their last? And why did that notion cause her such dismay?

...

Robert studied the financial reports. He was in the Marquess of Wendover's study, and the meeting had been arranged for the day after his wedding.

He set the pages aside. "Delmont's income from his properties and investments do not equal his spending."

Wendover rested his forearms on the massive oak desk and steepled his fingers. "It appears the viscount is being reckless with his spending habits."

"He's arrogant to a fault. It will be his downfall," Robert said.

Wendover's brow furrowed. "And you found no evidence to indicate the secret group is selling inventions to foreign militia for profit?"

"No. I found a blank sheet of paper in one of his safes, but he had yet to compose a message. I also believe a new member, Mr. Henry Heinz, was inducted into the secret group."

"And what of Lady Sophia? I must say I was surprised when I received your missive requesting me to make the hasty arrangements for your nuptials at St. George's."

His thoughts turned to Sophia.

His wife.

She'd made a lovely bride. Her green eyes had shimmered in the light from the church's windows as she'd walked down the aisle. There hadn't been time for a proper wedding gown, but she'd looked beautiful in an ivory silk ball gown that hugged her curves. Despite her brave nature, she'd clearly been nervous throughout the brief ceremony. He'd struggled with the urge to sweep her into his arms, offer her comfort, and kiss her senseless.

After the wedding breakfast, they'd returned to his home and he'd wanted her with a startling hunger on their wedding night. He'd fantasized of opening her bedroom door, stripping her naked, spreading her glorious chestnut hair across the pillows, and burying himself inside her welcoming body.

Instead he'd isolated himself in his library with a bottle of whiskey. It wasn't until the first streaks of sunlight had shown through the window that he'd deemed it safe to sulk back to his bedchamber.

His musings were interrupted by Wendover's voice. "And how is Sophia handling the turn of events?"

"The wedding was unforeseeable," Robert said.

"But for you two to marry—"

"I never wanted her to accompany me," Robert said curtly.

"You blame me for the outcome?"

"The lady should never have been involved. Missions can easily turn deadly."

The marquess raised a hand. "No need to bring up the past. I supported your change of plans. However, this mission must be solved, no matter the price."

• • •

Sophia's clothing and personal items were packed and moved to Robert's home in Grosvenor Square. Robert's staff was clearly taken aback to learn that their master had married so quickly, but they efficiently saw to her comfort.

His home was even more luxurious than she recalled from her brief visit weeks ago. She remembered stepping inside the polished marble entry, and passing the elegantly appointed drawing room, music conservatory, and dining room. But she was even more impressed by the kitchen and scullery, which were scrubbed clean, and the basement, which was stocked with wine and coal.

Her bedchamber was far lovelier than the one she'd occupied in her father's home. Decorated in shades of rose with a window seat overlooking the back gardens, it was charming and spacious.

As for her husband, he'd been absent on their wedding night and the entire day after. He rose early and departed before she came down for breakfast, and he didn't return home until past midnight. She understood he was a busy man, but neither was she used to sitting about and she'd certainly never anticipated being ignored.

Was this part of his plan? To avoid her and assure a marriage of convenience? And what of the mission? Did he intend to keep her ensconced in his home and out of harm's way? He'd said they were to work together. Had he changed his mind?

The following morning, she rose at the highly unfashionable hour of seven, summoned her maid, and dressed quickly. She knocked on Robert's bedchamber door only to find the room vacant. Descending the grand staircase with purpose, she intended to have a word with her new husband. The smell of fried bacon and eggs alerted her to someone's presence in the dining room.

She stopped short upon entering the room at the sight of Robert sitting at the table, a full plate of eggs, bacon, and toast before him, reading the business section of the *Observer*. All she could see of him were his fingers as he held up the newspaper.

She stood in the doorway. "I was searching for you."

He lowered the paper and grinned. "Good morning, Sophia. You look lovely." He rose and politely held out a chair and waited for her to sit before returning to his own seat. "How have you been adjusting here?"

She glared at him. "I'm surprised at your concern. I haven't seen you since the wedding breakfast."

"I apologize. I understand circumstances may be difficult for you, but I want you to be comfortable in my home. Shall you require anything, you have just to ask. Mr. Burke will see to your needs," Robert said.

Her voice was hoarse with frustration. "The staff has been very accommodating, but my husband has not. Where have you been?"

"I've been meeting with Wendover."

"What did he say?"

Just then a maid entered carrying a coffee pot and a plate of eggs and bacon. Setting the food before Sophia, she poured a steaming cup of coffee and left as quickly as she had come.

Sophia waited until they were alone once again. "Well?"

A wry but indulgent glint appeared in his eyes. "I have other plans regarding the mission. I think we should have our first celebratory ball as a married couple. We'll need invitations, of course."

She looked at him in bewilderment. "Pardon?"

"Invitations for a ball. Despite the reading of the banns, we did not send out invitations and our wedding was conducted in haste, don't you agree?"

"I suppose…"

"We need to select the proper foolscap, nothing but the highest quality will do."

The thought clicked in her mind. "You mean to visit Sir Falk and Sir Maxwell's stationery shop?"

"You catch on quickly, my dear."

"When?"

He motioned to her plate. "How quickly can you eat?"

Chapter Twenty-Six

Falk and Maxwell's shop was located on Bond Street. Clouds blocked the morning sun and a distant rumble of thunder threatened impending rain. Milling pedestrians looked to the darkening sky and rushed inside nearby shops in anticipation of rain.

Robert clutched Sophia's elbow and stopped before an establishment with a hanging sign that read F & M STATIONERS. The shops bells chimed as they opened the door and entered.

Rows and rows of shelves stacked with reams of paper crowded the perimeter of the room. Tables with samples were situated in the center for a customer's perusal and displayed everything from creamy velum to rare-colored foolscap to the type of paper used by newspapers.

At the sound of the bells, a large man with a walrus-shaped mustache approached from the back. He smiled in greeting.

"May I be of assistance?"

"We are Lord and Lady Kirkland and are acquaintances of Sir Falk and Sir Maxwell. Are they present?" Robert asked.

"Alas, no. Sir Falk and Sir Maxwell no longer run the day to day business," the man said.

"We are newly wed and looking to send out invitations for our first ball. Nothing but the highest-quality foolscap."

"Of course. Our finest wove paper is in the corner." The shopkeeper picked up a piece of paper from one of the tables and held it to the light. "See the watermark 'F&M'?"

She accepted the sheet. She knew that wove paper was finer and more expensive than laid. Laid paper was made from a larger screen of brass wires that left an impression on the paper that could be seen when held up to the light. Wove paper used a densely woven wire screen to drain excess water from the wet rag pulp to produce a higher-quality paper with a smoother surface.

"If you choose to commission paper," the shopkeeper said, "a watermark displaying the Kirkland coat of arms can be created by weaving a design into the screen's wires."

"Where is the paper mill?" Robert asked.

"Our factory is at Princess Wharf in Wapping. Both Sir Falk and Sir Maxwell see to the production. They've also recently acquired a printing press." He waved his hand at the tables. "Please feel free to peruse all of our selections."

Robert went from table to table, picking up sheets of paper and making a show of holding them up to the light.

Sophia followed. "What are you looking for?" she whispered.

"A specific type of paper. I found foolscap in Delmont's

bedchamber safe. There was nothing written on it, and I initially thought he used invisible ink. But after trying several methods to read any writing I came to the conclusion that there was no message."

"Why would he have a blank piece of foolscap in his safe?"

"My thoughts exactly. We're going to find out."

They walked to the back of shop and came to a door that appeared to lead to a rear storage room. Robert turned the handle, but it was locked. "I'll have to pick the lock."

"You can't! The shopkeeper will catch us."

"Not here. There should be a door in the alley that will gain us access. We'll go around."

On the way back to the front of the shop, he grabbed a stack of paper from one of the tables and handed it to the shopkeeper. "These samples will do nicely." He paid for his purchase and they departed.

The air was hot and humid as they hurried down the alleyway to the back of the shop. The alley reeked of refuse and city. A stray dog with a mangy coat looked up from its meal of chicken bones. An empty crate with puffs of straw rested beside the back door.

This door was also locked. Robert thrust his new purchase at her and removed his lock picks from his coat pocket. In less than a minute, the latch clicked and he opened the door.

She didn't realize she had been holding her breath until she let it out in a great rush. Following him inside, she scanned the small, cluttered space.

A closet was in the corner, its door ajar, and a battered table was in the center of the room. Resting upon the table was a vat full of sodden rag pulp, a sponge, and a wood-framed screen. On the floor beneath a high window, were blankets of felt.

"The shopkeeper was wrong. They do make paper here," she said.

He shook his head. "Not machine made, but handmade paper the old-fashioned way."

He lifted the top blanket of felt to find a dried sheet of newly made paper. He held the sheet up to the window.

"I'll be damned," he said.

"What is it?"

"We've been wrong all along. They are not stealing military inventions. They're common thieves."

"Tell me."

"The paper." He continued to study the sheet. "It's similar in color, size, and weight to the paper in Viscount Delmont's safe."

"So?"

"It's very specific. The feel. The texture. The color. The distinguished swirls. It's wove paper, not laid. It's a work of art and finely made. Only an expert papermaker could produce such quality. All that's missing is a watermark."

"What does it mean?" she asked.

"Shut your eyes and touch it." He handed the paper to her.

She closed her eyes and ran her fingers up and down the length, then crosswise. "It feels like…like a banknote."

"Exactly."

Her eyes flew open. "Good Lord! You mean they are forging banknotes?"

"If my theory is correct, then yes. They are not after their members' inventions, but their different skills."

"But forgers need more than just paper," she insisted.

"They need an expert engraver to replicate banknote plates and they need a press."

"The shopkeeper said Falk and Maxwell recently acquired a printing press. As for an engraver...Mr. Brass," she said amazed.

"It makes sense. I suspect Brass had an episode of conscience and sought to leave the group, but the mastermind could not risk him exposing their scheme," Robert said.

"What about my father? The other members who were murdered?"

"Your father and the others must have learned the truth. They were silenced before they could report it to the authorities."

"Henry Heinz did have a stack of banknotes beneath his mattress," Sophia said.

"And I found stacks of banknotes of varying denominations in Delmont's safes. But we need solid proof."

"We need to find the forged plates," she said. "Mr. and Mrs. Brass are on their way back to London so Mr. Brass can see his own physician. Mr. Brass may keep the plates in his shop."

"No. The plates won't be in Brass's shop," he said. "They will be at Maxwell and Falk's factory. They have everything they need there—the plates, the special wove paper, and the printing press."

"Then we must visit—"

She was interrupted by the excited barking of the stray dog in the alley. A split second later, a man cursed outside the door, then a *crash* resounded and the dog yelped.

Robert pointed to the closet. "Inside. Quick!"

She rushed to obey as he tucked the sheet of paper into his coat pocket, then joined her in the closet. The space was tight with shelves crowded with bins of rags and more reams of paper. They were pressed tightly together, and Sophia was aware of the coiled tension in Robert's frame. The closet door was cracked open, giving her a limited view of the room. She listened in horror at the sound of the back door handle turning.

A man stepped inside. He was tall, built like an ox, with a bald pate and a short upper lip. He rummaged around, muttering under his breath, as he added torn bits of rag to the vat.

Her heart pounded. The burly man went to the blankets of felt beneath the window. He picked up the top piece, then froze.

Her stomach clenched. *He knows one is missing!*

His beady eyes scanned the room and settled on the closet. He stalked over just as Robert shoved the door open, hitting him in the forehead and catching him by surprise.

Robert moved fast, with a punch to the stomach and a jab to the chin. The man's head snapped back. He stumbled, hit his head on the corner of the desk, and went down hard.

Robert's expression was fierce as he dragged the man by his booted feet into the alley with Sophia following. It had started to rain and her dress soon became damp. He searched the man's coat and quickly emptied his pockets. Coins, a pound note, and a pocket watch followed.

She stepped close. "What are you doing?"

"It must look like he was set upon by a thief."

Once again he was quick to react—just like he had aided her when Mr. Brass had been attacked.

Robert stood and grasped her hand. "Let's go."

He ushered her down the alley to the closest cross street. Within minutes they were in his carriage. Leaning against the cushioned seat, she brushed tendrils of wet hair from her forehead. "Heavens! Do you do that often?" she asked.

"Only when necessary."

"Remind me never to anger you."

He frowned at her. "It's not me you need to fear."

"I want to go with you to the factory."

His lips curved into a smile. "Wasn't this enough excitement for you?"

She met his blue gaze. "You should know me better by now."

. . .

Sophia lay in bed that night and allowed her subconscious thoughts to surface. It was clear by Robert's actions that he intended to keep physical distance between them and seek out Gareth Ramsey's services after the mission was completed.

But the problem was that she was unsure. More and more she admired Robert, was drawn to him, and if she was truthful to herself…desired him. And why not?

They were husband and wife.

She stared at the door separating her bedchamber from his, and every fiber in her body hummed for the pleasure of his touch.

For him.

A low *thud* sounded in the adjacent room. What the devil was that?

She rose and slipped on her wrapper. Perhaps he couldn't sleep either. Perhaps he was dreaming of her...

She reached for the handle and stepped into his room. Her eyes widened at what she saw.

He was thrashing on the bed and had knocked over a book on an end table. He was dressed only in his trousers, and a sheen of perspiration covered his bare chest. His expression was one of anguish. He was muttering, clearly in the middle of a horrid nightmare.

She rushed to the bed and shook his shoulder. "Robert! Wake up."

It was more difficult to rouse him than it had been the last time at the Delmonts' country home. When he finally woke, his eyes were unfocused and his breathing labored.

"Sophia," he simply said, his brilliant blue eyes staring up at her.

She smoothed his brow. "It was just a bad dream, Robert. Only a dream."

"Only a dream," he muttered.

He breathed deeply, the corded muscles of his throat and chest glistening in the candlelight. He was a strong man, capable of cracking safes and taking down large guards, yet he was clearly vulnerable and tormented. Her heart lurched at his distress.

She sat on the bed beside him. Reaching out, she cradled his face with her hand. His eyes were haunted, and she instinctively sucked in a breath.

"Don't pity me," he said in a choked voice.

He tried to turn away, but she held him firmly. "Tell me what happened the day Gwendolyn died."

"I can't."

"Tell me."

"You'll look at me differently. I can't bear that."

"No. I won't. Trust me."

"I told you she died during one of my missions."

"How?"

Silence lengthened between them, and she feared he wouldn't answer.

"It was a cold December night. I was camped outside the home of the Comte DeForte, a double agent and traitor to England. My mission was to blow open his safe, steal treasonous documents, and assassinate the Comte."

He hesitated then as if she would cringe at the thought of him killing another. She squeezed his hand, encouraging him to continue.

"I waited for hours in the bushes. The explosives were in place. The Comte's carriage arrived and just as he stepped down I lit the fuse. But then another person descended… Gwendolyn. I couldn't stop the fuse in time and the explosion tore her apart."

Her heart ached for him. "Was Gwendolyn an agent for the Crown as well?"

He laughed a bitter sound. "God, no. Gwendolyn disapproved of my occupation. She didn't believe in war, espionage, or revenge…only peace. She even thought the Napoleonic Wars could have been diplomatically settled. I promised her I would resign after I completed my last mission."

Sophia's brow furrowed. Gwendolyn sounded completely different from herself. Sophia wanted Viscount Delmont to pay for his crimes, and if he died, then so be it. But Gwendolyn sounded truly unselfish.

"Why was Gwendolyn with the Comte DeForte that

day?"

"She was with the Comte to save me. A traitorous Englishman had sold a list of all English spies and their immediate family members to the enemy. DeForte had somehow tricked Gwendolyn into meeting him in order to save me."

"It wasn't your fault."

He shook his head. "I set the explosives. I lit the fuse."

"It wasn't your fault. You were carrying out your assignment."

He looked at her in amazement. *"I murdered her."*

"No. You were tricked along with Gwendolyn."

"It doesn't matter. I was unworthy of her. Just as I'm unworthy of you."

"Listen to me," she said, her tone sharp. "You are not unworthy. You save people's lives. You saved *my* life."

"You don't understand—"

She kissed him then. Kissed him with all the pent-up emotion she felt. Her heart skipped a beat as she finally acknowledged that she loved him, knew it with every fiber of her being. She loved this strong, tortured man who blamed himself for past deeds in which he was just as much a victim as others.

His hands tightened on her shoulders as if he would push her away, but he moaned low in his throat and held her to him. Her palms flattened against his muscular chest, and she pushed him down on the mattress and lay atop him.

They were both urgent in their need, undressing quickly. The feel of skin against skin was enthralling, sending desire pooling low in her belly and between her legs. He kissed her breasts and stroked the curve of her hips. Then he slid his hand between her legs, and she gasped as he slid a finger deep inside her.

"Take me inside you," he said, shifting her until her legs straddled his hardness.

She lowered herself, anointing the tip of his manhood with her slick arousal.

"Sweet Jesus." He moaned.

He thrust forward until he was buried to the hilt in a raw act of possession. They both cried out, the pleasure was so intense.

With his hands on her hips, he showed her how to ride him. She was quick to learn, and met his thrusts in uncontrolled passion. Her head fell back, her breasts arched forward, and her body blossomed from the pleasure. He cupped her breasts, teased her tightened nipples with his teeth, and a moan of ecstasy slipped through her lips as the sensations built to a heightened pitch.

His hand slid down her belly and between her legs. His thumb caressed her sensitive bud and the hot tide of passion raged through her body. He pulled her head down for a searing kiss, and his tongue slid in and out of her mouth just as he plunged deep inside her.

Her body peaked and exploded. Her inner muscles clenched until he stiffened and spilled his seed inside her.

Exhausted, she fell against him and his arms came around her. She nuzzled his chest and inhaled his masculine scent. His heart beat strongly beneath her cheek. Thoroughly exhausted and satiated, she slept.

Chapter Twenty-Seven

Robert held Sophia tenderly as she slept. He gazed in wonder at her face, her kiss-swollen lips, and the chestnut tresses across his pillow. No one had ever taken such care of him. He was amazed that she'd still wanted him after he told her of his sordid deeds. For the first time in years, he felt worthy.

She shifted against him. They were married; he could hold her all night and no one would protest.

Ah. To keep her forever as his wife.

He'd never contemplated the thought after Gwendolyn. But Gwendolyn was far from his mind. They hadn't shared this blistering passion, this intellectual connection. Gwendolyn had wanted him to change, wanted him to stop spying for the Crown. She had never wanted to acknowledge or hear of his past. She was innocent and naive; he'd never been able to share his deepest secrets with her.

Sophia was different. He might have taken her innocence,

but she was far from naive and she possessed an admirable determination and shrewd intelligence. She accepted him for who he was; his faults and his dark past did not repulse or frighten her, and, amazingly, her trust in him hadn't faltered.

Somehow she had enraptured him. She'd come to him tonight and he'd been lost—all coherent thought had fled in a rush of desire. He hadn't withdrawn from her silken heat. She could be pregnant. The thought of her carrying his child should strike him with fear.

It should, but shockingly it didn't.

He trailed a finger down her shoulder and arm, marveling at the satin texture of her skin. Her eyelids fluttered open, and she smiled up at him.

"I want to show you something," he murmured close to her ear.

"Now?"

"Yes." He sat up, suddenly feeling like an eager schoolboy.

"But it's the middle of the night and I'm not dressed," she protested.

He chuckled. "It doesn't matter. We're married now, remember?"

He drew on a dressing gown and helped her with her nightgown and wrapper. Retrieving a candlestick, he opened the door and took her hand in his.

• • •

Sophia giggled as they descended the grand staircase and wove through a myriad of halls. "This feels like a grand adventure."

Robert stopped outside a closed door and reached

for the handle. The door swung open to reveal an empty room. Moonlight streamed in through four large windows and illuminated the space. She tentatively stepped inside. It wasn't empty as she'd initially thought—packed trunks and crates were stacked in the far corner.

"What is this place?" she whispered.

"Your new workshop."

She gasped and stepped farther into the room. She saw it then. Her father's scarred worktable was set up against the far wall. She hurried to the closest trunk and threw open the lid to find her tools. Nestled in crates lined with straw were dozens of her glass beakers.

She whirled to face him. "You had this room emptied out and my belongings moved here?"

His lips curled into a smile and he nodded.

She still couldn't believe it. It was a spacious room, larger even than her father's workshop. The tall windows would allow for plenty of natural sunlight while she worked. "You did this? For me?"

"I want you to be happy here," he said.

She swallowed a lump in her throat. He had been thoughtful enough to spare a room and designate it as her workshop. She'd never been allowed her own space when her father was alive.

"I realize you may not be here forever, but I promise to have everything moved to wherever—"

She threw herself into his arms, cutting him short. His lips met hers halfway. She didn't want him to finish his thought, and there was one sure way to distract him. She parted his robe and ran her hands down the slabs of muscle beneath.

...

The following morning, Robert helped Sophia out of the carriage in front of Maxwell and Falk's factory. A large brick building in the east end of London, the factory was nestled between warehouses along the docks. Tall ships were anchored in the distance, the stench of the river was strong, and the occasional squawking of seagulls could be heard.

The factory's looming front door was made of solid oak. She would have struggled with the weight if Robert hadn't held the door open for her to pass. As soon as they stepped inside, the sounds of machinery and men's voices could be heard from deep in the recesses of the building.

"Stay close to me." He took her hand.

Factory workers rushed to and fro. A hand-cranked paper-making machine dominated the floor. Its long wire screen moved through a large vat of pulp suspended in water until a thin coating settled onto the screen. Enormous rollers squeezed out the excess water, and the damp paper was rolled up on an end to dry.

A man carrying a heavy sack threw fistfuls of torn bits of rag into the vat. Another stirred the thick soup of pulp.

Nobody paid Sophia and Robert any attention. They watched the paper-making process until they spotted Sir Maxwell's tall frame beside Sir Falk's short, portly figure at the far end of the building. By their wild hand gestures and furrowed brows, it appeared as if the partners were in heated debate.

"The animosity remains between the business partners," Robert drawled.

Just then, Sir Falk turned to motion to a nearby worker when he noticed Sophia and Robert. He said something to Sir Maxwell and the pair started toward them.

"Let me do the talking," Robert told her.

Sir Maxwell reached them first. "Lord Kirkland. What an unexpected surprise."

Sir Falk approached and bowed to Sophia. "Lady Kirkland, I understand congratulations are in order for your recent nuptials."

"Thank you."

"To what do we owe the honor of your visit?" Maxwell asked.

"We visited your stationery shop for commissioned paper and the clerk informed us that you spent your time here."

"Ah, yes. We can show you our special stock in my office," Sir Falk said, steering them away from the machine and into their private office.

She knew the forged plates had to be here. But with Falk and Maxwell present, they would never be able to search the warehouse.

They spent the next hour going over the paper with the business partners. A Kirkland coat of arms was drawn for the watermark and the precise wording of their so-called invitations decided upon.

She shifted restlessly in her seat and glanced at her husband beneath lowered lashes. He appeared relaxed and leisurely, intently concentrating on the stationers' every word.

Robert leaned back in his chair. "I had inquired about a print shop, but the clerk at your shop told me you had recently acquired a press."

Falk glanced at Maxwell before answering. "It's true."

Robert was right! *They have everything they need,* Sophia thought. *The paper, the engraved plates, the printing press.* She wanted to jump up and run to the nearest constable.

Yet Robert merely smiled, appearing greatly pleased at this bit of news. His blue eyes were completely unreadable, the inner workings of his mind indecipherable.

She wasn't fooled.

Not for the first time, she marveled at his ability to hide his emotions and his private thoughts.

...

Once they were back in their carriage, Robert turned to Sophia.

"I'll have to return at night," he said.

She leaned forward in her seat, her pink lips parting. "Do you need to go back? Isn't what we saw sufficient enough?"

"No. I must connect Viscount Delmont and the secret group to the counterfeiting scheme. And I still need to find the forged plates. I suspect they plan a delivery very soon."

Her green eyes widened. "How do you know?"

"The preparation of the special paper. And Maxwell and Falk couldn't get us off the factory floor fast enough. My guess is they are counterfeiting one hundred or fifty pound notes so as not to draw unwanted attention to themselves."

"You were right then. There is no military espionage. Delmont, the mastermind, and the secret group are nothing more than thieves," she said.

"Yes."

"It explains everything. The viscount's lavish lifestyle. The Inventor Society's unlimited funds for its members like Henry Heinz. My father and the others must have suspected the truth, and they were murdered for it."

"It's a likely scenario."

She sucked in a breath. "These are dangerous men."

"All my missions are dangerous." He regretted the words as soon as they left his lips. Her face paled, and she looked like she was going to protest.

"Robert?"

"Yes."

Her eyes glistened with unshed tears. "Please be careful. I've come to…to care for you."

He kissed her then; he couldn't help himself. Her lips trembled beneath his and it took all his will not to press her back against the leather bench and slide his hand beneath her skirts, trail his fingers up her silken legs.

He sat back instead. "Don't worry, Sophia. This is what I do."

She nodded bravely and bit her bottom lip.

His gut knotted. "I'll drop you off at home. I need to inform Wendover."

•••

Robert met Wendover in a private corner of a coffee shop on Fleet Street. He'd wasted no time in informing his superior of his theory.

Wendover's brow furrowed. "Counterfeiting is a serious offense against the King. You must be able to prove it."

"Now that I know the truth, I won't be misled searching Delmont's safes and pursuing a wrong theory. The entire house party was a wild-goose chase," Robert said.

The marquess sipped his coffee. "And you believe George Brass, a common jeweler and silversmith, talented enough to engrave counterfeit plates?"

"He's not a common jeweler. He works with his hands every day and deals with precious metals. His wife claims he is a talented engraver and can copy famous works of art," he said.

Wendover sighed. "If the bankers and the public learn of counterfeit banknotes, it could cause wide-spread panic."

Robert set his coffee cup down. "That's what Haverton and his fellow murdered inventors knew. Delmont and the mastermind had them killed to keep their secret."

"What's your next move?"

"I'm setting a trap tonight at Falk and Maxwell's factory."

The marquess leaned close. "What do you need from me?"

"Two armed men to wait outside for my signal."

"I'll arrange for it."

"There's something else," Robert said. "I need to you to look after Sophia while I'm gone. She worries unnecessarily."

"Of course. I'll pay her a visit."

Robert nodded. "I'll find sufficient evidence to incriminate Delmont and put an end to the secret group's agenda. And I expect to unveil the identity of the mastermind. One way or another, this mission will come to an end."

Wendover regarded him gravely. "Then you'd best proceed with caution."

• • •

Sophia stood in Robert's bedchamber as he slipped a wicked-looking blade into his boot. He was dressed entirely in black, with form fitting trousers, Hessians, and a jet lawn shirt. The dark color made his sapphire eyes shine like a midnight sky.

When he was finished, he looked at her. "It's time," he said simply.

Her heart beat rapidly. She didn't want him to go, didn't want him to face danger. Unspoken words lodged in her throat and she swallowed.

She nodded and followed him out of his room to the top of the landing. Her fingers clung to the ornate gilt railing leading down to the marble vestibule.

He turned to leave.

"Wait!" she cried out.

He walked back to her and cradled her cheek with his hand. "We've been over this. I'll be back before sunrise."

Despite her resolve to be strong, her voice wavered. "I know. It's just…I want to go with you."

He chuckled softly. Placing a finger under her chin, he tilted her face upward. "As soon as I find the plates, I'll send a signal to Wendover's men, and we can go and arrest the guilty parties."

She took a deep breath, then blurted out the words. "I love you."

His expression shifted, an almost imperceptible flicker of emotion crossed his eyes.

Had she made a mistake? Should she have kept quiet until after tonight's mission? She didn't want to disrupt his concentration.

He slowly leaned forward and captured her lips in a gentle kiss that left her weak with longing.

Lifting his head, he kissed her forehead. "I'll be back."

Chapter Twenty-Eight

Robert blended with the shadows against the east side of the paper factory. Unlike this morning, the front door was locked. With his tools, he pried open a casement window and slipped inside the building.

He lowered himself and landed agilely on his feet. He lit a candle from his coat pocket, and his eyes adjusted to the glow. The large rollers of the paper machine loomed before him. Stacks of felt were laid out on long tables.

Crouching low, he stealthily crept through the building. He needed to find the printing press, where the forged plates would most likely be located. Crates of paper loomed in haphazard piles throughout the bowels of the factory. Several minutes later he located the press—a seven-foot-long handpress with a flat stone bed.

He lifted the press's platen, and his heart pounded at the discovery of two expertly engraved plates for the front and back of a hundred-pound note. He couldn't help but admire

Mr. Brass's workmanship. The forged banknotes he had encountered in the past were shoddy and easily detectable as forgeries, but these…

Every detail was meticulously copied from the signature to the serial number to the date. Combined with the high-quality wove paper, the forgeries would be excellent.

Beside the press was a stack of wove paper that was similar to the paper that had come from the vat that both he and Sophia had found earlier at the stationers'. He held a sheet up to the candle's light.

His pulse raced. This paper had a watermark that repeated six times and read "The Bank of England." Once the paper was fed through the printing press and carefully cut, each sheet would yield six banknotes.

A perfect scheme. But when did they plan on delivering the forged notes?

At the sound of the front door opening and voices, he slipped behind a shelf stacked with reams of paper and extinguished the candle.

"Everything is ready." He recognized Maxwell's voice.

"We ran into no problems." Falk's voice.

They carried lanterns and set them down upon crates. Robert shifted to the side and glimpsed Viscount Delmont's large frame through a space between the reams. A film of sweat covered Delmont's face, and he paced back and forth before the press.

"The delivery must be exactly as ordered," Delmont said, wiping his forehead with a handkerchief.

Robert pulled his pistol from his coat pocket. Wendover's men would be in place by now. Soon he could return to Sophia. Hold her in his arms. Tell her his true feelings for her...

"His lordship's orders are precise. He is expected shortly, and we cannot afford another incident," Delmont said tersely.

"There won't be another," Falk said.

His lordship? They must be speaking of the mastermind. *At last*, he thought. *Let the villain show himself!*

...

Sophia gave up pacing her bedchamber and went downstairs to her new workshop. She ran her hand over her father's scarred worktable and breathed deeply. She planned to unpack boxes and crates and lose herself in her work while she waited for Robert to return. She'd never needed a distraction so badly.

She started with her father's tools, his hammers, wrenches, screwdrivers, and jars of nuts and bolts. She arranged them upon the table in order by size and importance. She had just dragged over a crate and started removing the fragile glass beakers when there was a light knock on the door.

"Yes."

The door opened and Mr. Burke stood in the doorway. "The Marquess of Wendover is requesting to speak with you."

Her first thought was terrifying. What if something had happened to Robert? "Send him in at once," she said.

The butler must have sensed her alarm, for seconds later the marquess strode into the workroom.

"Sophia!" he said.

She flew to him and embraced her father's old friend. "Why are you here? Is it Robert?"

The marquess pulled his mouth in at the corners. "Don't worry. Nothing's happened to Robert. I've come to offer you comfort. I knew you'd be worried, and I was right. I want you to accompany me to my home until tonight's events have passed."

"Are you certain all is well?"

"All will be. Trust me. Now go fetch your cloak. My carriage is out front."

Minutes later, Wendover escorted her into his waiting carriage. Leaning back against the leather bench, he regarded her thoughtfully. "I was good friends with your father, you know."

"I know, my lord."

His eyes were shadowed by thick brows. "I was just as upset at his passing as you."

She didn't think anyone could have been as upset as his only child, but she held her tongue. He was acting out of sorts tonight, but then perhaps the stress was affecting him as well.

She glanced out the window just as the driver turned a corner, heading into an unfamiliar part of the city.

She frowned. "I thought we were going to your home."

"We need to make a quick stop first."

"Where?"

The carriage had passed the last town house and left the residential neighborhood. Without the hustle and bustle of pedestrian traffic, the streets were eerily quiet, until the distinctive stench of the river wafted through the window. A sliver of moonlight reflected off the water, illuminating the masts of tall ships.

She blinked in surprise. "We're headed for the docks?"

"Yes."

"Robert is in danger then!"

"Not yet, my dear, but soon."

More than just his tone was strange now. "What on earth do you mean?" She whirled to face him and was shocked to see him holding a pistol, the barrel aimed at her chest.

Her unease exploded into alarm. She gasped as a heart-wrenching awareness struck her. "You! You're the mastermind!"

"You always were too astute for your own good, Sophia."

"But you're Robert's superior at the Home Office. You work for the Crown!"

"And I will continue to do so once he is disposed of."

"And what about my father? You were supposed to be his good friend."

His lips thinned with a cynical twist. "I was. I offered him admittance in our secret group. I even had a gold gear made for him and he snubbed me. I had no choice but to have him disposed of. And you," he said, pointing a finger at her. "You are just like him, too righteous for your own good. He could have been as wealthy as Croesus, he could have had unlimited funds for his inventions, could have hired assistants to aid him in his workshop. But did he listen to me? No! He threatened to expose me, expose everyone involved. I had no choice."

"You had him murdered!"

His features twisted into a maddening leer. "As his offspring, you turned out to be just as meddling. You were supposed to be in prison for the attack on George Brass, but I should have known Robert would come to your aid. He was always very resourceful."

A flash of pure rage ran down her spine. "You're nothing

but a greedy thief. A murdering, greedy thief."

His eyes narrowed. "You know nothing, my dear."

To her horror, he pulled out a length of rope from beneath the seat and laid the pistol on the bench. Before she could lunge for the weapon, he grasped her arm in a painful grip and yanked her close.

She fought fiercely, kicking and scratching. He grunted as she kicked his shin and landed a blow on his ear, but his strength overpowered hers. He tied her arms behind her back and stuffed a gag in her mouth.

The carriage came to a stop and the door opened. He dug the pistol into her side. "It's time, Sophia," he said as he hauled her out and dragged her inside the factory.

· · ·

Robert remained crouched behind the tall shelf while observing the three men.

"Open this one," Delmont ordered, pointing to a crate that had been nailed closed.

Falk rushed to comply and Delmont held up a bundle of banknotes. "Beautiful, aren't they?" he said in a reverent tone as he raised the banknotes to his nose and made a show of smelling them.

"Let's get them out of here," Maxwell said.

"Not until his lordship arrives," Delmont said.

Robert's pulse quickened. He raised his pistol and stepped into the light. "Shall we wait together until his lordship arrives?"

The three men whirled at the sound of his voice. Falk and Maxwell looked paralyzed with fear.

Viscount Delmont's lips curled in a slow smile. "Well, well. I was wondering how long it would take for you to make an appearance tonight."

Maxwell and Falk exchanged stunned looks. Robert read them instantly; they had no idea of his involvement. But Delmont appeared to know and a prickle of unease pierced his spine.

"It's over, Delmont. Armed men are waiting outside. You'll be arrested and tried for your crimes and so will your ringleader as soon as he shows his face," Robert said.

Delmont laughed. "I wouldn't count on it, Kirkland."

Again Robert's instincts heightened and he turned at the sound of a scuffle of footsteps on the wood floor. A muffled groan followed.

His eyes widened in alarm as the Marquess of Wendover came into the light hauling a gagged and bound Sophia behind him. He held a pistol to her side.

"You should listen to the viscount, Robert," Wendover said.

Robert's gaze flew from Wendover to Sophia. Her green eyes were wide with fear, and his heart stopped.

He turned to the marquess. "Tell me it's not true."

Wendover's face was hard, cruel, and pitiless as he thrust Sophia onto a crate and pointed his pistol at her head. "I'm afraid it's true." With a jerk of his head, he motioned to Robert's pistol. "Now drop your weapon or she's dead."

Robert had little choice but to comply and he slid his weapon across the wooden floor. He glared at Wendover with murderous fury. "Why?" he demanded.

"Sophia stated it quite bluntly in the carriage ride here. Greed. The opportunity presented itself; it was the perfect crime. The talent offered in the Inventors' Society was unparalleled. Mr. Brass's engraved plates are better than the Crown's master plates, and Maxwell and Falk's paper is indistinguishable from any official banknote."

Delmont, sneering at Robert, approached with a length of rope. He bound Robert's hands behind him and shoved him onto another crate, back-to-back with Sophia.

As soon as they touched, he felt Sophia tremble. He feared Wendover would kill her, and his gut twisted. He couldn't live through the murder of another of his wives, and Sophia's death would be a thousand times worse than Gwendolyn's. Sophia was his heart's desire, and he couldn't… *wouldn't* allow her to come to harm.

Reinforcements weren't coming; he was on his own. He had to distract Wendover…buy himself time.

"Why assign me the mission?" Robert asked. "Why have me look into the Inventors' Society if you were the mastermind after all?"

Wendover regarded him solemnly. "I had no choice. The secretary of the Home Office was demanding answers for the death of the inventors, including the Marquess of Haverton." He glanced at Sophia. "I had to think of something and what better way than to connect the deaths to a secret group who stole their inventions and sold them to foreign militias for profit? I never thought you would discern our true counterfeiting scheme."

"You thought wrong."

"An unfortunate turn of events." Wendover glanced at Maxwell and Falk. "You two can go." For once, the business partners didn't argue but rushed toward the exit.

He doesn't want witnesses, Robert thought.

He knew Delmont had been in deep debt and in need of funds to effectively run the Inventors' Society and maintain his lavish lifestyle.

But Wendover? No one knew much about the marquess's personal life.

Robert's gaze narrowed upon his superior. "What about patriotism for your country?" he said tersely.

"Napoleon is defeated. I did my duty," Wendover said. "You don't believe in patriotism either. You were going to leave the Home Office after you married Gwendolyn. I couldn't allow it."

A feeling of cold dread settled in Robert's chest. "What are you saying?"

"You forced me to send Gwendolyn to DeForte that day. I couldn't permit you to resign. I counted on you seeking revenge after her death, but you stubbornly insisted on leaving. It took a threat to one of your father's friends to entice you back into espionage."

Robert's vision tunneled until all he could see was Wendover through a red haze of hate. He jerked against his bindings, his heart hammering. His lips peeled back from his teeth and he growled low in his throat. He wanted to attack like a wild animal, gravely wound the man he'd thought of as a close friend, his superior at the Home Office, who had betrayed him so badly.

Someone firmly grasped his bound hands.

Sophia.

He became aware of her fingers urgently clutching his. Through sheer force of will, he took deep breaths and calmed his pounding heart. Now more than ever before he needed to concentrate, needed all his cunning and skill.

Sophia's life was at stake.

Wendover and Delmont turned away to inspect the contents of one of the crates. Robert seized the opportunity, straining against his bindings once more—no longer in a rage—but in a calculated effort to reach into his boot. His fingers grazed the hilt of his blade.

Time was running out.

Chapter Twenty-Nine

Sophia felt Robert strain to the side and immediately understood his intent. The knife he'd stashed in his boot.

Let me, she wanted to whisper, but the gag was firmly in her mouth.

Wendover and Delmont were both occupied removing counterfeit banknotes from the crates and stuffing them into a canvas bag. Sophia shifted to the side and reached the blade in Robert's boot.

She was sweating as her fingers twisted and sliced at Robert's bindings. With her hands bound behind her back, it was hard work. Several times the knife slipped and she feared she would cut him or drop the blade. Her efforts were finally rewarded when he snapped the frayed rope just as she was halfway through his bindings.

Pivoting quickly, he removed the gag from her mouth and cut her bindings. He held a finger over his lips and mouthed, *Stay still.*

Their task completed, Wendover approached holding the pistol. Delmont stood behind him with a bag of banknotes slung over his shoulder.

"Robert, I'm disappointed that our working relationship must end this way. But again, you leave me no choice. I'll see to Sophia first," Wendover said.

She watched in horror as Wendover pointed the pistol at her belly.

Robert launched himself at him and the men wrestled for the pistol. Robert's knife clattered across the floor. Delmont leaped at Robert, grabbing him from behind in an attempt to yank him away from Wendover. Robert struck out and swept Delmont's knee, causing all three men to go down in a fighting heap. A lantern was knocked aside, igniting the canvas bag of banknotes.

She watched in horror as the fire spread across the wooden floor, consuming the straw-stuffed crates.

Good Lord! The factory was packed with reams of paper, and within no time the place would go up in flames.

The pair of villains continued to fight Robert. Delmont punched Robert in the face, and Sophia screamed. She leaped forward, balling her fists and hitting Delmont on the back. The viscount twisted to look at her with a surprised expression before he struck her across the temple. Pain shot through her head and she landed hard on the floor. She raised herself on her elbows just as Delmont reached for Robert's knife.

She scrambled to her feet, frantically searching for a weapon when she spotted the engraved plates. Lifting one high, she ran at Delmont and smashed the heavy steel onto his head with all her might. There was a sickening *crunch*, and the viscount dropped the knife and collapsed.

The blast of a pistol exploded in her ears. Her breath caught in her throat.

Please don't let it be Robert!

Seconds passed, an eternity, and Robert stood. Blood stained Wendover's shirtfront.

"Quickly!" Robert shouted. "This place will be an inferno in less than a minute."

The path of flames had already widened, eating up the wood floor. He grasped her hand and pulled her behind him. The air was thick with smoke as they sprinted through the maze of the factory toward the door.

Once outside, he clutched her shoulders. "Sophia, love. Are you injured?" His expression was one of heart-wrenching concern and fear.

Her throat ached and her voice wavered. "No…I'm fine."

"Let's get away from here."

She glanced inside the factory. Flames consumed the interior and heat blasted her face. The two men inside would never survive.

She covered her mouth with her hand, and they fled into the night.

. . .

Robert hailed a hackney cab, helped her inside, and gave the driver directions. As soon as he settled on the bench, he enveloped her in a strong embrace. She was trembling, an aftermath to their close escape.

"What will happen?" she said. "With both Wendover

and Delmont dead and the factory burned to the ground?"

"Don't worry. The Home Office will concoct a story."

"But how—"

"Shhh. You're shaking like a leaf and in shock. Let's get you inside."

She was slow to realize the hackney had arrived outside their home. He carried her inside and up the stairs to her chambers. He dismissed Burke and her maid along the way and slammed the door shut with a booted foot. Setting her down on the edge of the bed, he knelt before her.

His blue eyes were brilliant as he gazed at her. "My God. I almost lost you," he said, his voice full of despair. "It would have been my fault. Again."

"No. You couldn't have known about Wendover."

"He was going to take you from me. I couldn't bear it."

She cradled his face with both hands and forced him to look in her eyes. "He didn't. You saved me. I love you, Robert."

He tenderly trailed a finger down her cheek. "Sophia, my love…my wife. I love you with all my heart. It's *you* who saved *me*. I was lost without you. A cold, bitter man wandering from mission to mission. You gave me hope and love and a second chance at life. Without you, my life has no meaning."

"Oh, Robert. I thought you were going to send me away."

"Never, darling. Will you stay with me as my wife?"

Her heart leaped with joy. "Yes! Oh, yes."

He swept her into his arms and cradled her against him. "Thank God."

She drew his head down to hers and told him just how she felt with a passionate kiss. He returned the kiss deeply, while gently driving her down onto the pillows. A jolt of excitement shot through her at the brush of his arousal against her belly. Sliding her hand between their bodies, she caressed him.

"Ah, my love." He groaned. "You've been through a traumatic evening. You need to rest."

"Later," she murmured. "I need my husband now."

He was blissfully quick to oblige her. A short time later he was sliding into her and she was trembling with ecstasy as they joined not just their bodies, but their hearts.

Chapter Thirty

Two nights later, Sophia woke alone bed. Memories of the night of the warehouse fire were still vivid in her mind. Since the frightful ordeal, she'd had difficulty falling asleep. But Robert had held her tenderly at night and whispered love words in her ear until she'd slept.

Glancing at the mantle clock, she realized it was late morning. She dressed and hurried to the library where she found her husband sitting behind his desk, reading correspondence.

He rose and drew her into his arms to kiss her, lingeringly and sweetly. Her senses spun.

"I have something to show you," he murmured against her lips.

He turned to the desk and handed her a copy of the *Times*. She frowned as she glanced at the front page. Then her eyes widened as the article caught her attention.

"Read it out loud," he urged.

She cleared her throat and read:

The tragedy at the Princess Wharf paper factory was an alleged act of arson. The owners of the factory, Sir Falk and Sir Maxwell, were suspected of counterfeiting banknotes. The unfortunate deaths of two respectable gentlemen who were investigating the forgers, the Marquess of Wendover and Viscount Delmont, have been reported as casualties of the fire. The Ordinance Department has sustained a loss with the death of the Marquess of Wendover. The London Inventors' Society is grieving the loss of its leader, Viscount Delmont. Falk and Maxwell are currently in Newgate awaiting trial at the Old Bailey.

She looked at him in surprise. "This article is hardly accurate."

"The secretary of the Home Office has decided to keep the surreptitious criminal acts of Wendover and Delmont a secret. By blaming the counterfeiting on Maxwell and Falk, the conspiracy has been foiled. They've been stripped of their titles and their royal warrant as stationers for the Crown."

"All the loose ends are tied nicely," she said.

He watched her intently. "Delmont dies a hero. Are you upset not to see justice served for your father's murder?"

She folded the paper. "I admit that I'm disappointed. But I'm also confident that Delmont will be judged by his maker. He cannot harm anyone else."

"The Home Office shall survive this setback as well," he said.

"And you? Aren't you angry that Wendover was never

charged with treason? Especially after what happened to Gwendolyn?"

"Surprisingly, no. It's in the past. I have much to look forward to."

"Will the Home Office ask you to return?"

He shook his head. "I suspect Gareth Ramsey and Daniel Forster will be called to duty. Both are more than willing to take my place in espionage. Besides, I'm needed here."

"Ah, as the Earl of Kirkland?"

His blue eyes twinkled with mischief as he embraced her. "No, as a devoted husband. I suspect all my prior missions will fall short in comparison."

She shot him a saucy look. "Truly? I was thinking that we should continue to work together. As spies, that is. We make a wonderful team. You wouldn't want to get bored, would you?"

"Bored? With your inventions and our future children, I expect to be kept quite entertained and busy."

She put her arms around his broad shoulders and pressed against him. "I shall work hard to keep it exciting."

He sighed and tangled his fingers in her hair. "I suspect it won't be difficult for you."

She licked his lower lip and gently nipped it. "It shall be great fun. A grand adventure."

He chuckled as he lowered his mouth to hers. "And that's why I love you."

Author's Note

The practice of locksmiths placing ads to anyone who could pick their locks was common. The Joseph Bramah lock mentioned in my book as "Impregnable as the Rock of Gibraltar" did indeed exist. In 1811, Braham offered a reward of two hundred guineas to anyone who could successfully pick the lock. In 1851, a man by the name of Charles Hobbs managed to pick the lock after working tirelessly for four hours per day for ten days. Hobbs was then hired by the Chubb Company, which soon became the top lockmaker in England.

I hope you enjoy reading my book as much as I have enjoyed writing it!

Acknowledgments

Thank you to my agent, Stephany Evans, for her wonderful insight and help. Thank you to Maryliz Clark, the best grammar queen in New Jersey.

And a special thank-you to John and my family for all their support. I couldn't have done it without you.

About the Author

Award-winning author Tina Gabrielle is an attorney and former mechanical engineer whose love of reading for pleasure helped her get through years of academia. After multipublishing for a prestigious law journal, she fulfilled her dream of writing fiction. She is also the author of adventurous Regency historical romances, *In The Barrister's Bed, In The Barrister's Chambers, Lady Of Scandal*, and *A Perfect Scandal* from Kensington Books.

A Spy Unmasked is the first book *In The Crown's Secret Service* series. The second book in the series, *At The Spy's Pleasure,* is coming soon from Entangled Publishing.

Tina's books have been Barnes & Noble top picks, and her first book, *Lady Of Scandal*, was nominated as best first historical by *Romantic Times Book Reviews.* Tina lives in New Jersey. She loves to hear from readers. Visit her website to join her newsletter and enter free monthly contests at www.tinagabrielle.com

Manufactured by Amazon.ca
Bolton, ON